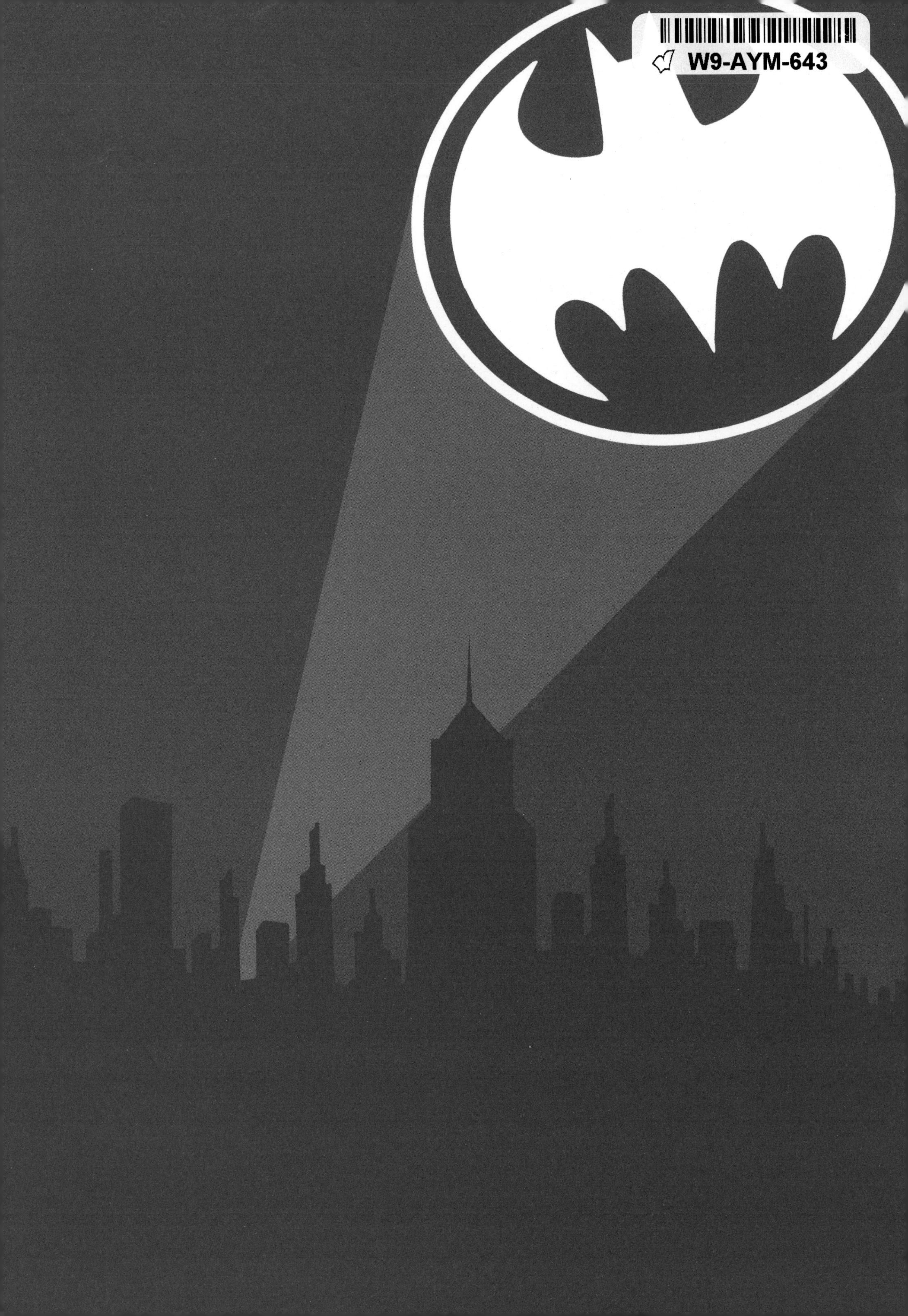

5-MINUTE BATMAN STORIES

™

ADAPTED BY DONALD LEMKE
BATMAN CREATED BY BOB KANE

HARPER FESTIVAL
An Imprint of HarperCollinsPublishers

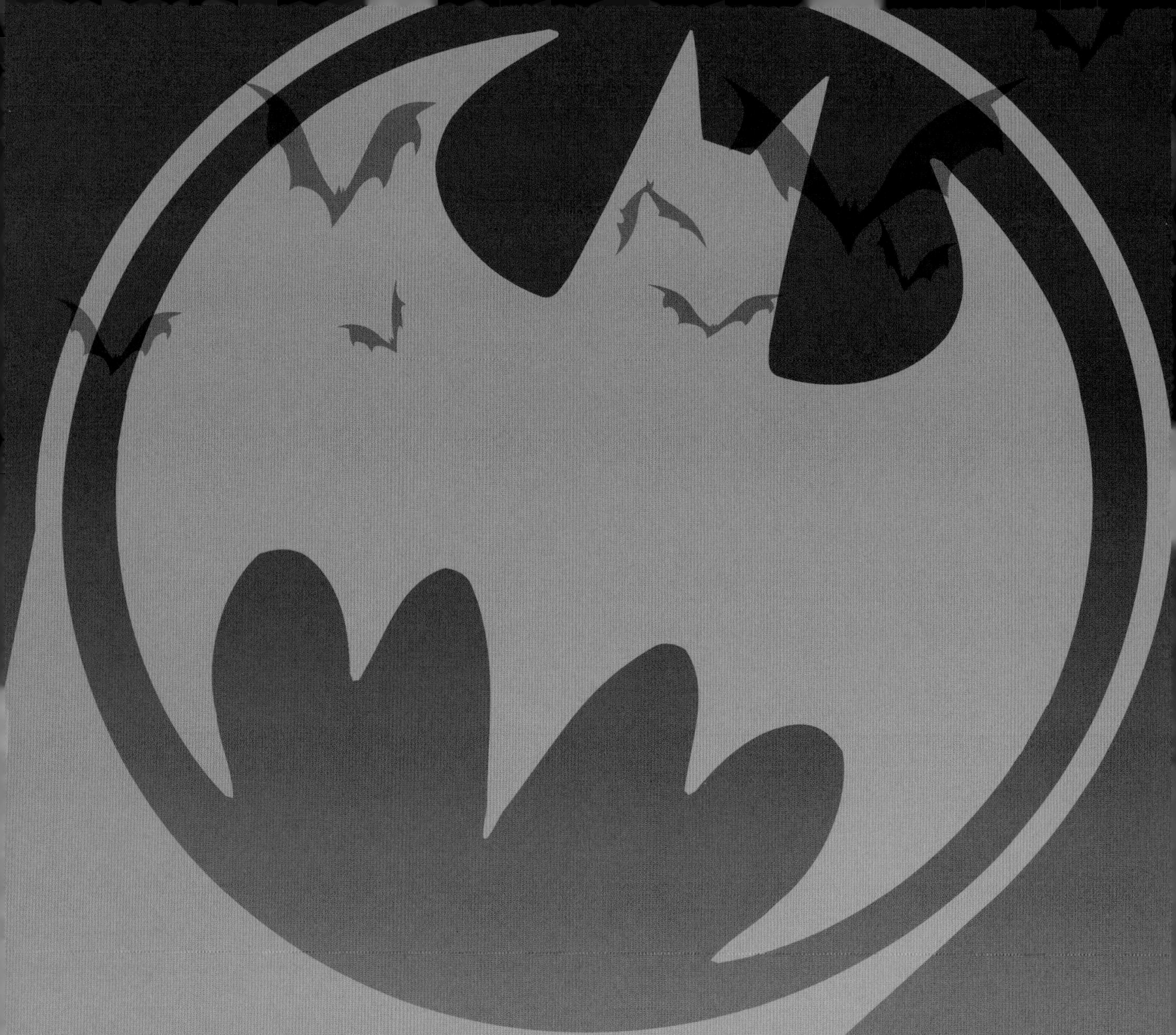

HarperFestival
is an imprint of HarperCollins Publishers.

The World's Greatest Heroes Unite originally published as *Meet the Super Heroes* written by Michael Teitelbaum. Illustrated by Steven E. Gordon.
Dawn of the Dynamic Duo originally written by John Sazaklis. Illustrated by Eric A. Gordon.
Professor Pyg's Circus Crime originally written by John Sazaklis. Illustrated by Jeremy Roberts.
Harley Quinn's Perfect Prank originally written by John Sazaklis. Illustrated by Jeremy Roberts.
The Tomb of Eternal Life originally published as *Eternal Enemies* written by John Sazaklis. Illustrated by Andie Tong.
The Penguin's Birds of Prey originally published as *Fowl Play* written by John Sazaklis. Illustrated by Steven E. Gordon. Colors by Eric A. Gordon.
The Joker's Night of Fright originally published as *Fright Club* written by John Sazaklis. Illustrated by Andy Smith. Colors by Jeremy Roberts.
Reptile Revenge originally published as *Reptile Rampage* written by Katharine Turner. Illustrated by Steven E. Gordon. Colors by Eric A. Gordon.
The Joke's On Who? originally published as *Battle in Metropolis* written by John Sazaklis. Illustrated by Andy Smith. Colors by Brad Vancata.
Batman and the Toxic Terror originally written by Jodi Huelin. Illustrated by Steven E. Gordon.
The Prince of Puzzles originally published as *Batman versus the Riddler* written by Donald Lemke. Illustrated by Steven E. Gordon. Colors by Eric A. Gordon.
Battle in the Batcave originally written by Donald Lemke. Illustrated by Andie Tong.

HARP33479
Manufactured in China. For information address HarperCollins Children's Books, a division of HarperCollins Publishers, 195 Broadway, New York, NY 10007.
www.harpercollinschildrens.com
Library of Congress catalog card number: 2014958870
ISBN 978-0-06-235798-4
17 18 19 SCP 10 9 8 7
❖
First Edition

TABLE OF CONTENTS

THE HEROES AND VILLAINS IN THIS BOOK!

HEROES

Batman

Knight

Batgirl

Nightwing

Batwing

Robin

Batwoman

Squire

Chief Man-of-Bats

Superman

Commissioner James Gordon

Wonder Woman

VILLAINS

Bane

Lex Luthor

Rā's al Ghūl

Catwoman

Mad Hatter

The Riddler

Harley Quinn

The Penguin

Scarecrow

The Joker

Poison Ivy

Talia al Ghūl

Killer Croc

Professor Pyg

Two-Face

BATMAN™

THE WORLD'S GREATEST HEROES UNITE

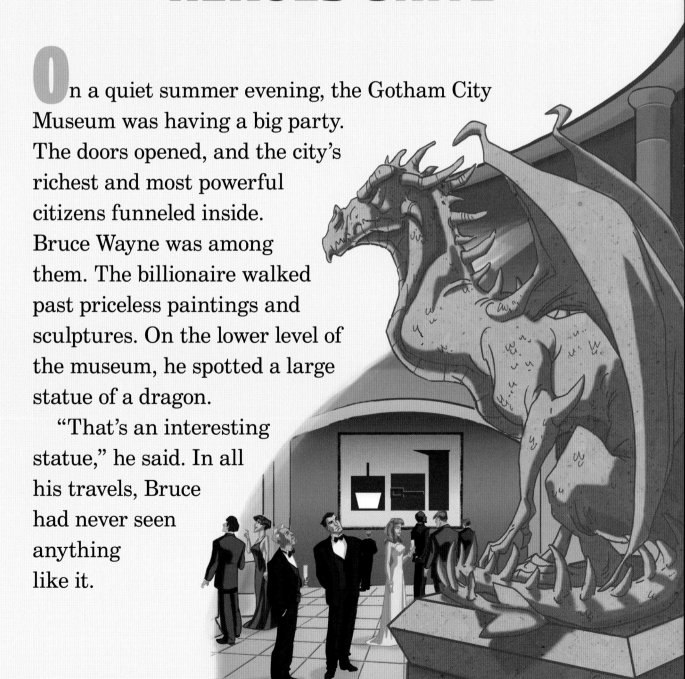

On a quiet summer evening, the Gotham City Museum was having a big party. The doors opened, and the city's richest and most powerful citizens funneled inside. Bruce Wayne was among them. The billionaire walked past priceless paintings and sculptures. On the lower level of the museum, he spotted a large statue of a dragon.

"That's an interesting statue," he said. In all his travels, Bruce had never seen anything like it.

Suddenly, the dragon statue came to life! Stone fragments rained down as the dragon flew into the air and shot fire from its mouth. People screamed and raced toward the museum exits as fast as they could.

"How did this happen?" Bruce wondered aloud as he ran outside with the other guests. "Someone's got to stop that dragon!"

Back at Wayne Manor, Bruce quickly headed deep below the mansion and entered the Batcave. The underground hideout contained high-tech vehicles, weapons, a computer, and the uniform of Bruce's secret identity—Batman.

Bruce quickly changed into his cape and cowl. As
Batman, he climbed into the Batmobile and raced back
to the museum. As he sped down the city streets, the Dark
Knight spotted the Bat-Signal. When the city was in danger,
the signal appeared in the sky, letting Batman know he was
needed. He saw the dragon flying overhead. The beast clawed
at skyscrapers and spit fire.

The Dark Knight quickly stopped the Batmobile and exited the vehicle. Using his Batrope, he scaled the city's tallest building. Then Batman took a Batarang from his Utility Belt. He threw it at the dragon with all his might.

The Batarang was hooked to a wire. As the Batarang flew through the air, the wire wrapped around the dragon. "Now I've got you!" Batman said.

Chomp! Chomp! The dragon bit through the wire easily with its large, sharp teeth. It swatted Batman away with its tail.

"I can't stop it alone," the super hero said as he dodged another attack. "I'm going to need some help!"

Batman quickly grabbed his sonic-wave device from his Utility Belt. The device gave off a high-pitched sound. It was a sound that only one man could hear.

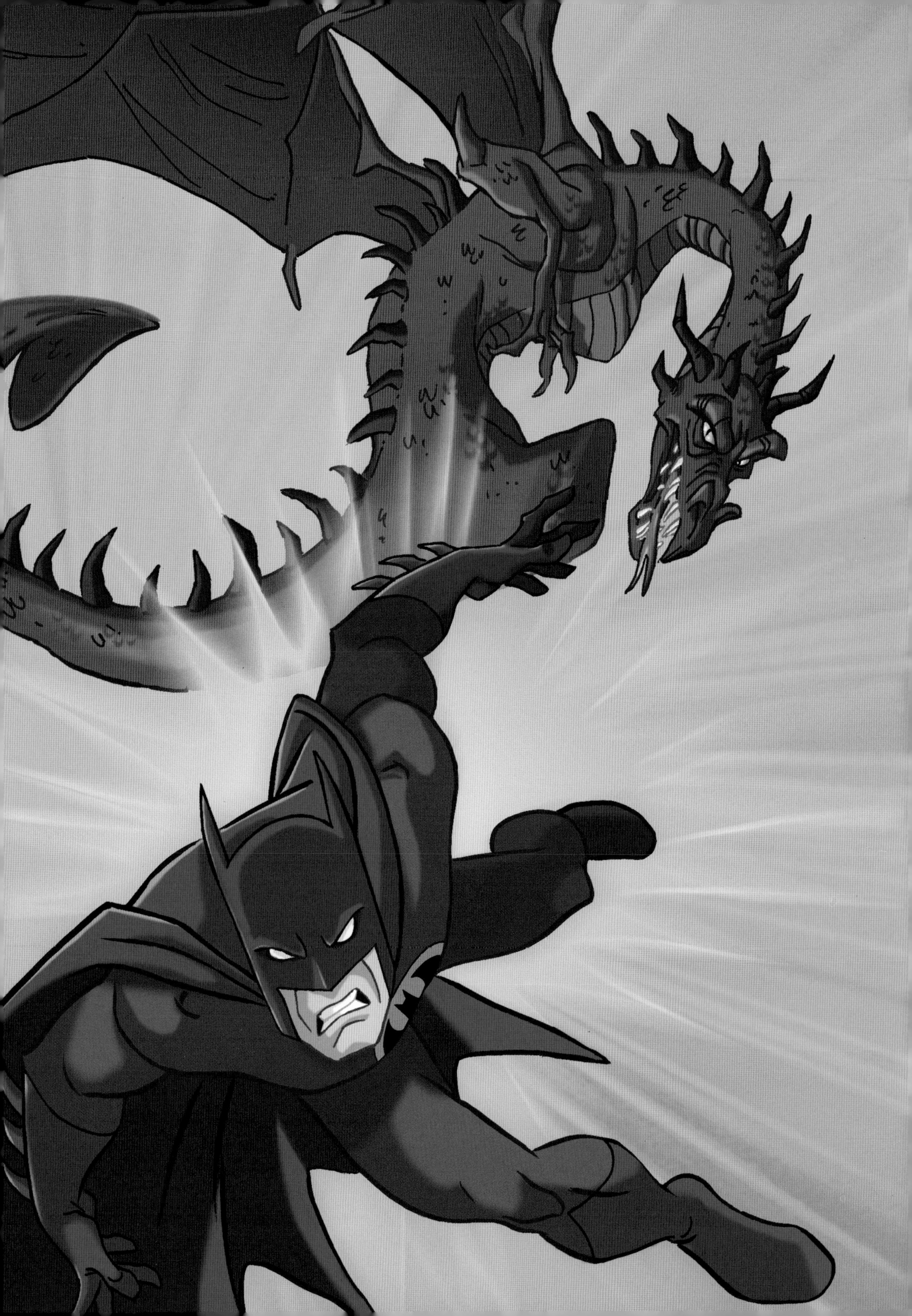

Miles away, Clark Kent was at work. He was a reporter for the *Daily Planet* in the city of Metropolis. His super-hearing picked up Batman's signal.

"Batman is in trouble," he said. "I'll have to fly at super-speed to get to Gotham City in time."

Clark quickly headed into a private closet. He removed his tie and glasses. Then he tore open his shirt, revealing his super hero uniform beneath. Clark Kent was Superman!

Superman arrived in Gotham City a few minutes later.

"Batman, what happened?" he asked his fellow hero.

"I'm not sure," Batman replied. "But there is a dangerous dragon flying around the city. It must be stopped!"

"I'll use my super-strength to catch the beast," Superman said.

Superman soared into the sky. When he was close enough to the dragon, he grabbed the beast's tail. *Fwhoosh!* The dragon shot a stream of fire at the hero.

"The dragon must have been brought to life by magic," Superman said as he dodged the flames. "My powers can't stop magic. We have to call Diana."

As she was leaving her office in Washington, DC, Diana Prince's phone rang. "Hello?" she said. She listened carefully while Batman explained what was happening in Gotham City. "I'll be right there," she said. Like Bruce Wayne and Clark Kent, Diana Prince also had a secret identity. She was Wonder Woman.

She quickly changed into her super hero uniform and took off in her Invisible Jet. "Statues just don't come alive and breathe fire," she said. "This sounds like dark magic!"

15

A few minutes later, Wonder Woman joined her friends in Gotham City.

"I have a plan," Batman said. He explained it to the other heroes. Then they jumped into action.

Wonder Woman twirled her Golden Lasso of Truth over her head. With a flick of her wrist, she threw the lasso at the dragon. It wrapped around the dragon's jaw, clamping the beast's mouth shut.

"Your turn, Batman," she called out.

With the dragon unable to shoot fire, the Dark Knight
approached with his steel cable at the ready. He quickly
wrapped the cable around the beast and pulled the
dragon to the ground. "You're next," he told Superman.

"This should cool you off," Superman said. Then the
Man of Steel used his freeze breath on the dragon.

The dragon struggled to break free, but it
couldn't move.

"Now what?" Batman asked. "Our binds won't hold the dragon forever."

Wonder Woman gently touched the dragon's snout. "I can link minds with the dragon," she said. "I can try to get it to reject the evil magic."

Using her special powers, Wonder Woman reached into the dragon's mind. Suddenly, the dragon vanished in a puff of smoke.

"Where did it go?" Superman asked, surprised.

"Follow me," Wonder Woman said. She soared into the air with the other heroes close behind.

Wonder Woman led Batman and Superman
back to the Gotham City Museum. The dragon
statue was back on its pedestal in one piece.
Their plan had worked!

"Good job, Wonder Woman," Superman said.

"I couldn't have done it without both of you," Wonder Woman replied.

"Thanks to you two, Gotham City is safe again," Batman said.

"Thanks to all of us!" his friends replied. "We make a great team."

BATMAN™

DAWN OF THE DYNAMIC DUO

Perched atop a skyscraper, a dark figure stood watch over the night. Below, Gotham City was a dark and scary place, but this one man helped the police protect the innocent. He was a silent guardian. His name was Batman, the Caped Crusader.

Batman was really a billionaire named Bruce Wayne. He lived in Wayne Manor, a large mansion on the edge of the city. Underneath the mansion was Batman's secret hideout, the Batcave. This was where the Dark Knight kept the tools he needed to battle the crooks and villains of Gotham, including his high-tech vehicles and the Batcomputer, which helped him investigate Gotham City's criminals.

Batman couldn't protect the city alone, though. He had a sidekick named Robin.

Robin was a skilled crime fighter and a junior detective.

Together, Batman and Robin made up the Dynamic Duo.

Robin's real name was Tim Drake. Before he became Robin, Tim took an oath to become Batman's partner and to keep his secrets.

Tim trained for many months. He learned martial arts, gymnastics, and how to use different weapons. When Tim was finally ready, Batman gave Tim his Robin suit.

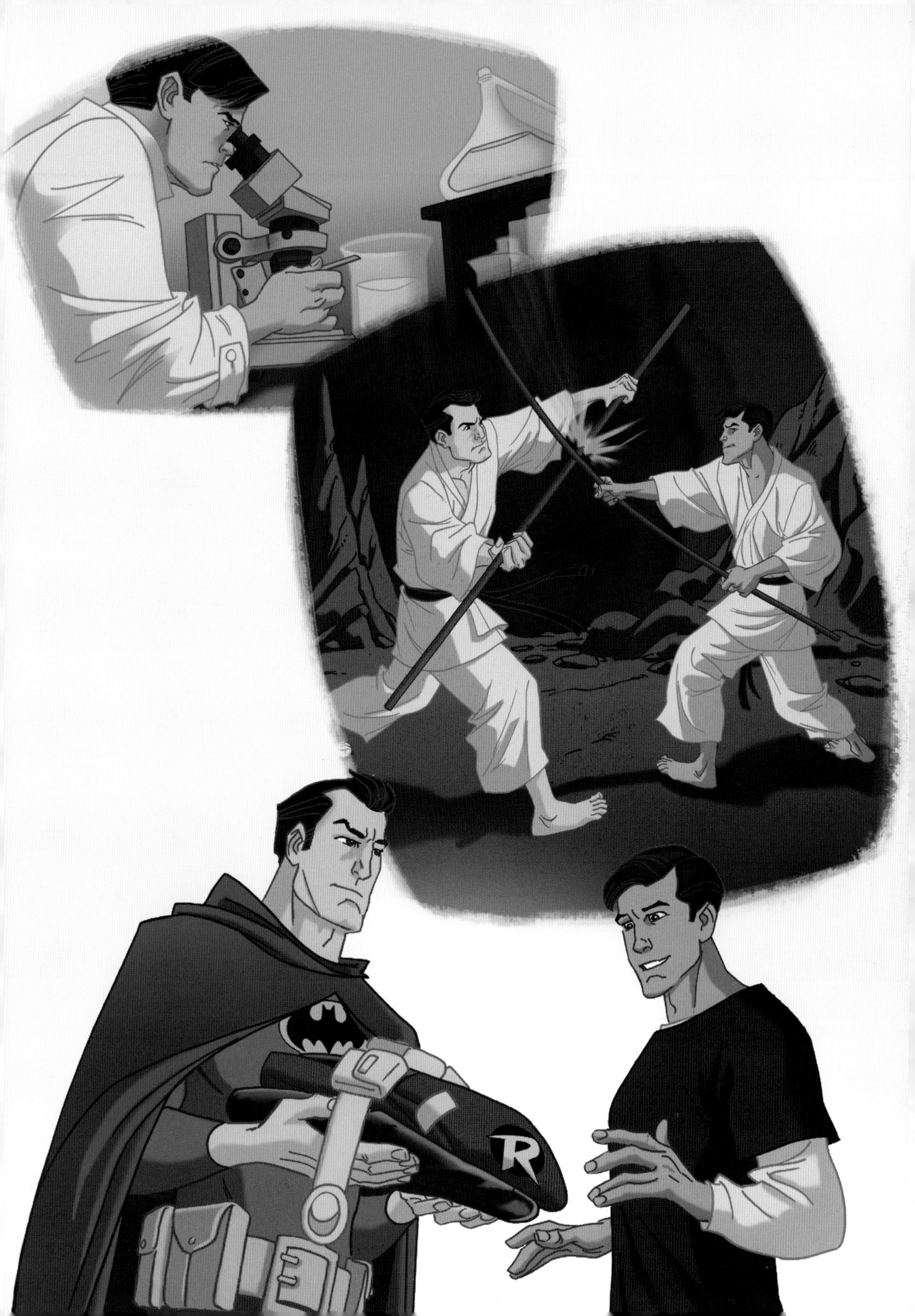

Tim Drake was not the first Robin to fight crime beside the Dark Knight. Batman's original sidekick was a boy named Dick Grayson. Dick, an orphaned acrobat, was taken in by Bruce Wayne. He was also trained to fight crime as Robin, the Boy Wonder. When Dick grew up, he became the hero Nightwing. Sometimes, he still helped Batman protect Gotham City.

Late one night, Bruce and Tim were in the Batcave when an alarm blared on the Batcomputer. There was trouble at the Gotham City Mint. A picture of the suspect suddenly appeared on the computer screen.

"It's Two-Face!" Tim yelled.

Batman and Robin put on their uniforms and armed themselves with many high-tech gadgets.

"To the Batmobile, now!" Batman said. The heroes hopped into the vehicle and zoomed out of the Batcave.

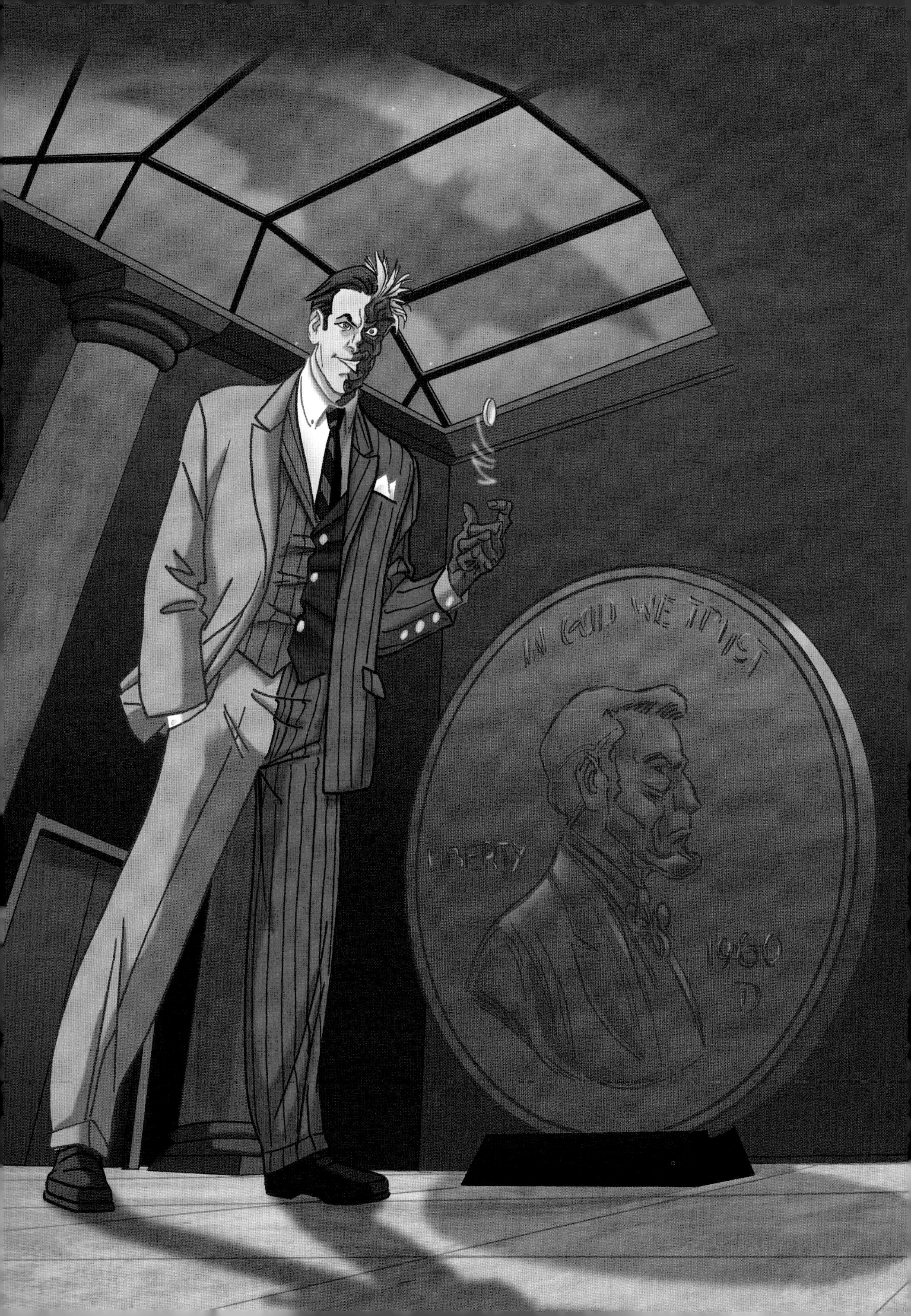
IN GOD WE TRUST
LIBERTY
1960
D

At the mint, the villain Two-Face flipped his favorite coin. "Heads, we steal half the cash. Tails, we steal *all* the cash!" the crook cackled. The coin landed in his palm. "This is our lucky day, boys," he said, looking down at the profile on his coin. "We're taking everything!"

His henchmen were known as the Two-Ton Gang. "You got it, boss," said one of the men, an evil grin on his face. The two strongmen easily broke into the vault using only crowbars and their incredible strength. The vault was filled with millions of dollars in newly printed bills and coins.

Two-Face led his henchmen into the vault. The villain dug his fist into a bag of coins, letting the pennies, nickels, dimes, and quarters fall through his fingers. "Who says change isn't easy?" Two-Face said with a laugh.

Suddenly, the Dynamic Duo smashed through a skylight above. Shards of broken glass crashed to the floor. The two super heroes swung to the ground on their Batropes.

"Drop the dough!" Robin said as he spotted the criminals.

"Heads up, boys," Two-Face shouted to his henchmen. "It's the bat and the brat!"

The two goons charged at the Dynamic Duo.

"Looks like you're in double trouble," Two-Face said to the duo.

Batman and Robin used their martial arts training to defend themselves against the crooks, but the evil men were too strong. After a long fight, the heroes were overpowered by the two henchmen.

Batman and Robin were each strapped to one side of the giant penny in the display.

"Let's break up the set," Two-Face snarled. "Flip the coin and flatten a foe! Which will it be—heads or tails, bat or brat?"

Batman spotted a familiar shadow hovering over them. "Don't be so smug," the Dark Knight said. "This isn't over yet."

Suddenly, a smoke bomb exploded inside the vault. The robbers were temporarily blinded by the cloud. They coughed and choked on the fumes. Ready for the surprise attack, Batman and Robin held their breath, protecting themselves from the toxic fumes.

When the smoke cleared, Batman and Robin were free. A new friend stood by their sides, ready to help defeat Two-Face.

"Nightwing!" the villain cried, recognizing Batman's former partner.

"The Dynamic Duo is now a triple threat," Nightwing said.

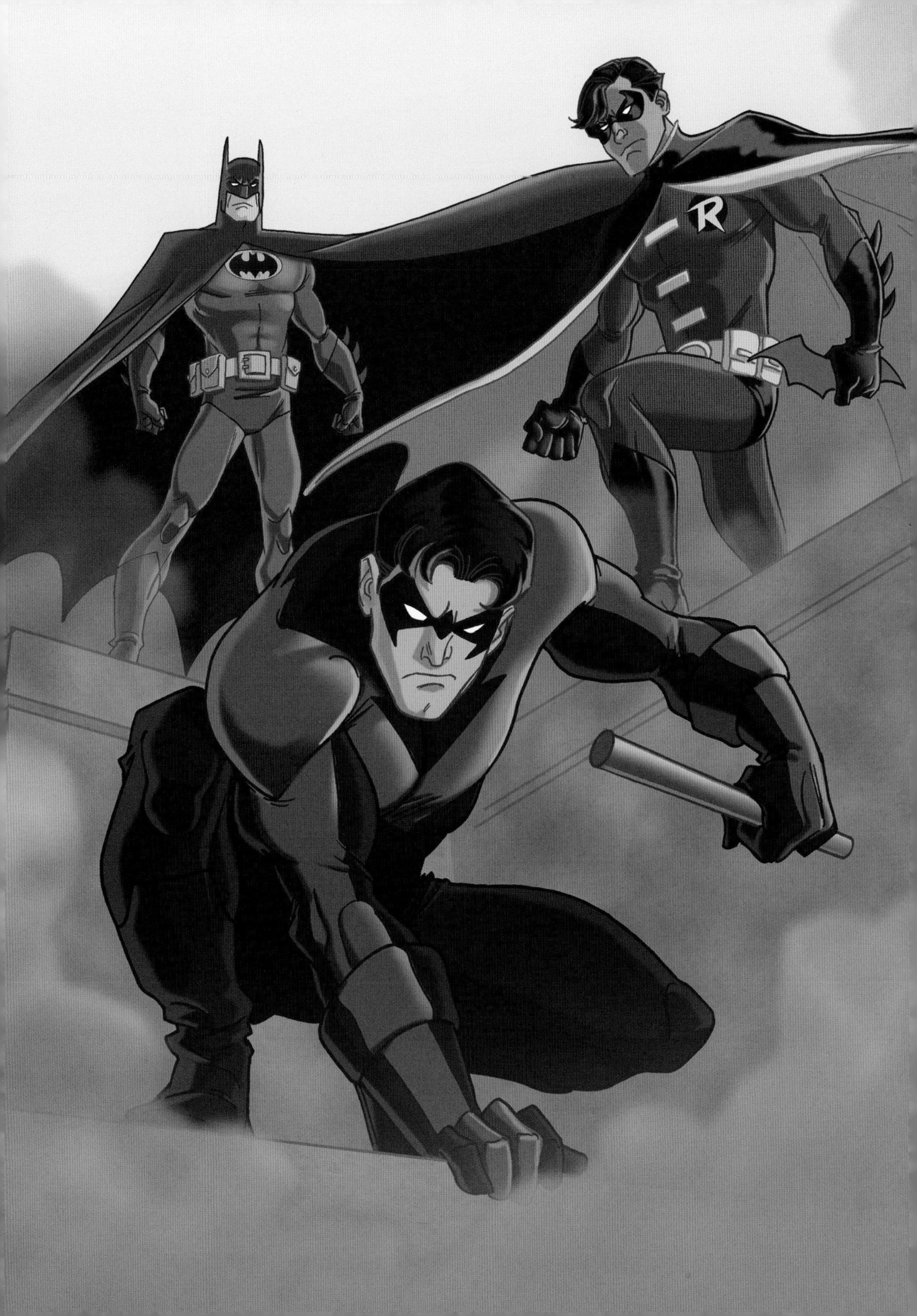

"Get them, you fools!" Two-Face yelled at his henchmen. The two crooks rushed at the heroes. Nightwing and Robin took on the thugs while Batman chased after Two-Face.

"Not so fast," the Dark Knight said when he caught up to the villain. With a gloved fist, he hit Two-Face with one swift punch. The villain fell to the ground with a thud.

Robin and Nightwing quickly defeated the others.

The Gotham City Police arrived and put the crooks in handcuffs.
Batman thanked Nightwing for his help.

"You're lucky I was in the area," Nightwing replied with a smile.
"I'm always glad to lend a hand." Then Nightwing turned to Robin.
"Batman has taught you well. You two are truly a Dynamic Duo."
Then Nightwing disappeared into the dark sky above.

"Nightwing is right. We got lucky tonight," Batman said. "We must keep training to stay smarter, stronger, and faster than our foes."

"Back to the Batcave?" Robin asked.

"Yes," Batman agreed. "Next time the Dynamic Duo flies, our enemies will be wishing for luck."

PROFESSOR PYG'S CIRCUS CRIME

Batman was the fearless guardian of Gotham City. High above the streets, he patrolled the rooftops in search of trouble or danger.

Suddenly, an alarm on his uniform sounded. Without hesitating, the super hero swung down from his perch on his Batrope. The Batmobile—a high-tech, armored, and voice-activated vehicle—waited on the streets below.

"To the Batcave!" Batman shouted, speeding toward his secret underground hideout.

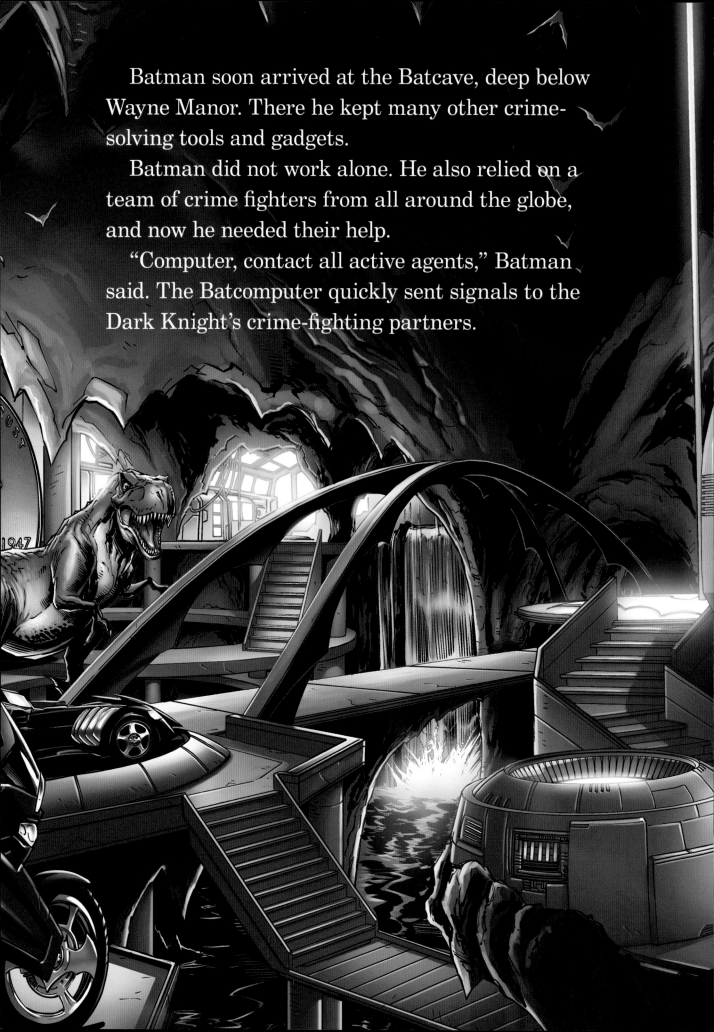

Batman soon arrived at the Batcave, deep below Wayne Manor. There he kept many other crime-solving tools and gadgets.

Batman did not work alone. He also relied on a team of crime fighters from all around the globe, and now he needed their help.

"Computer, contact all active agents," Batman said. The Batcomputer quickly sent signals to the Dark Knight's crime-fighting partners.

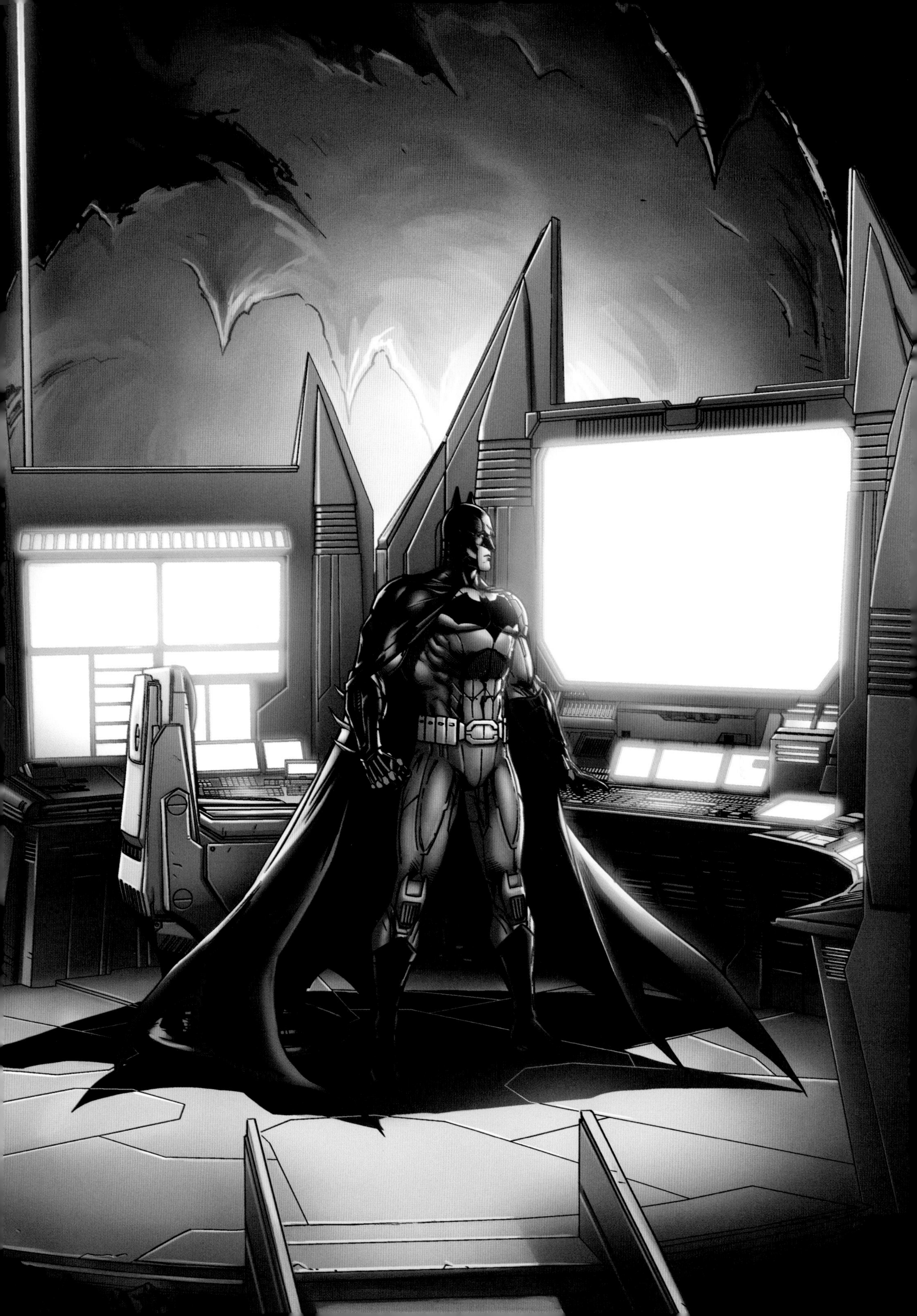

In England, Knight and Squire received Batman's signal. Knight had an armored suit made of heavy metal. His young sidekick, Squire, wore a colorful costume made to look like a court jester's. Both heroes were experts in combat and reliable friends of the Dark Knight.

Chief Man-of-Bats was a
Native American. He was
inspired by Batman to fight
crime. He had great skills
as a hero and a doctor.

Batwing was a
trained martial artist
from Africa. He had a
suit that used robotic
bat-like wings to help
him fly.

Once all of the agents were notified, Batman listened to the team's news. All of the heroes reported robberies in their cities. The Dark Knight discovered one common clue: the Circus of Strange. Batman also saw one other thing that was very interesting.

"The Circus is in Gotham City," Batman told his super hero team. "It's time for us to see the show."

All of the super heroes arrived in Gotham City. They gathered on the outskirts of the circus grounds to survey the area. The Circus of Strange was open for business, and people of all ages were enjoying the many sights and sounds.

The super heroes remained hidden from view as they planned their next move. Batman pointed to a tent set far apart from the other circus tents. It belonged to the ringmaster.

"Let's start there," the Dark Knight said.

Inside the circus tent, the ringmaster, Professor Pyg, stood inside a secret room surrounded by people. Like Professor Pyg, the others all wore masks to hide their faces.

The heroes quickly discovered that these people were circus workers who had been trained to be pickpockets! Their masks were really devices made to control their minds.

"Go forth, my Dollotrons," shouted Professor Pyg, "and bring me more riches!"

On Professor Pyg's command, the Dollotrons left the circus tent and moved through the crowd. They were sneaky and crafty. None of the other guests noticed that they were being robbed!

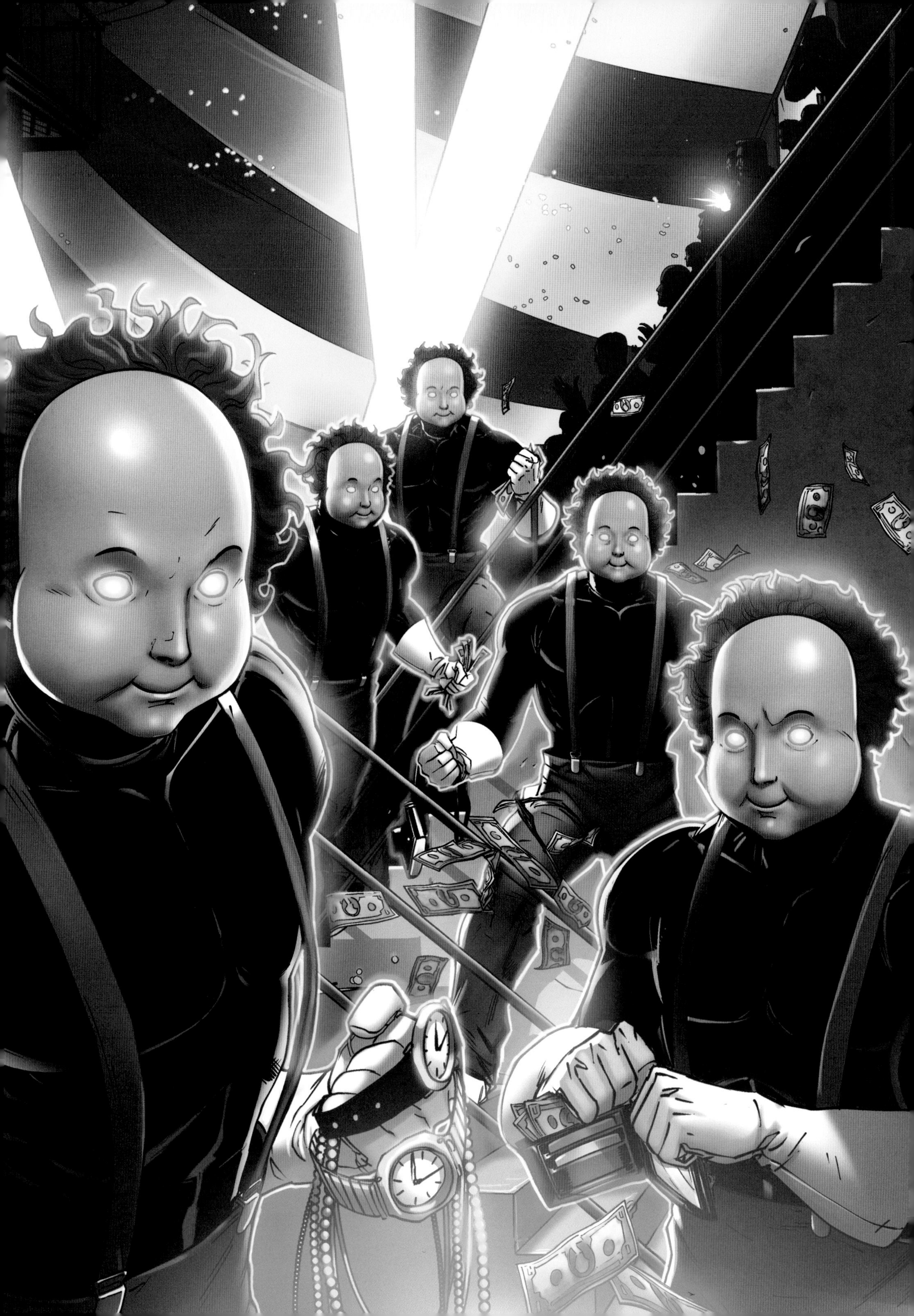

The super heroes watched from the shadows.
"We have to stop this evil scheme," Batwing said.
Batwing and Chief Man-of-Bats sprang into
action to round up the Dollotron pickpockets.

Meanwhile, the rest of the heroes snuck into a secret room of the ringmaster's tent to spy on Professor Pyg. Batman recognized the high-tech device the villain monitored. It controlled the masks the pickpockets were wearing.

The Dark Knight quickly formed a plan. He directed Knight and Squire to move silently through the tent and surround the professor.

"Hand over the cane, sir . . . ," Knight began.

"Or we'll make you squeal!" Squire finished.

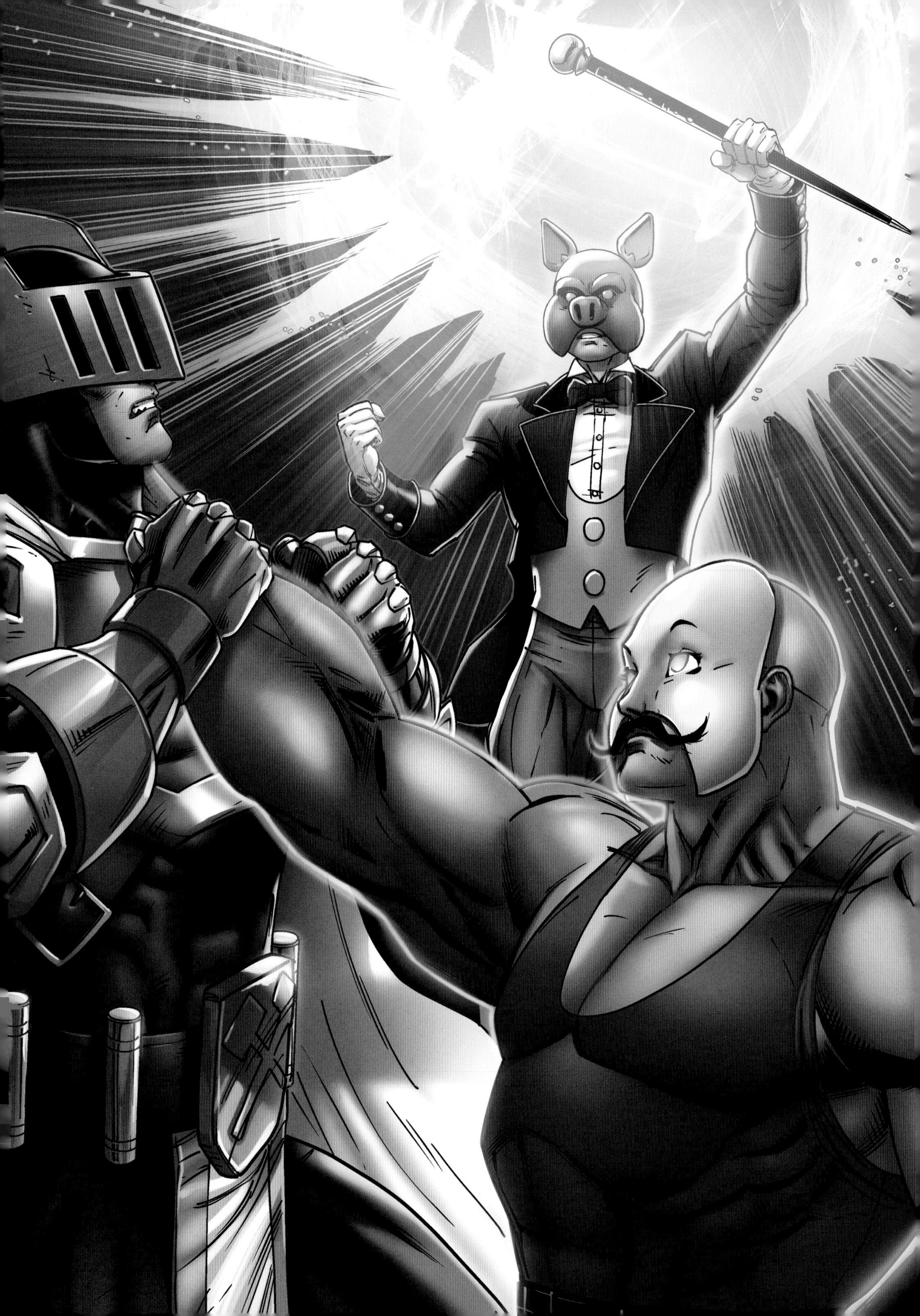

"Welcome!" Professor Pyg said to the super heroes. "You're just in time for the first act!"

The super-villain raised his cane into the air. The device exploded in a blast of green light, sending a shockwave across the entire circus grounds.

The circus strongman answered the super-villain's call. He wore a mind-control mask, too. He grabbed Knight and lifted the hero off his feet.

Squire quickly flew into action. She kicked the device out of Professor Pyg's hand, and the controller smashed to pieces.

The mind control
disappeared. The
strongman let go of Knight,
and Knight quickly knocked
him to the ground.

Now defenseless, Professor
Pyg made a run for the tent's exit.

"Not so fast!" shouted the Dark Knight. The caped hero
swung down from above and chased after the villain.

Batman twirled the Batrope above his head like a lasso.
With a quick flick of the wrist, he sent the ultra-strong wire
flying through the air. It wrapped around Professor Pyg, and
the Dark Knight pulled the wire tight.

"Looks like you're hog-tied now," the hero said.

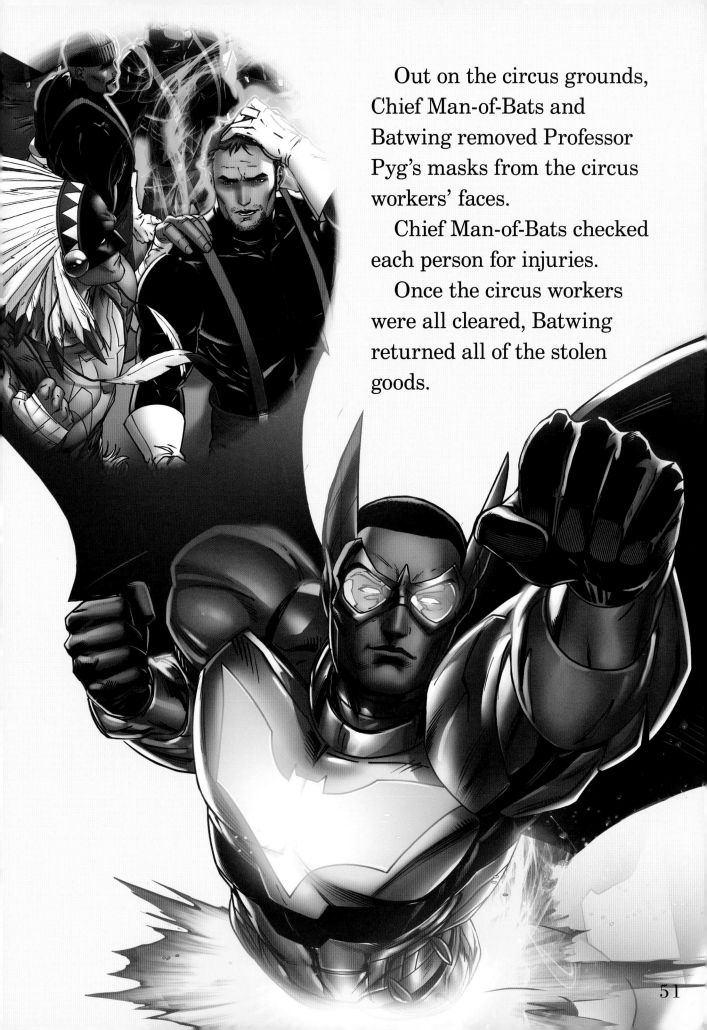

Out on the circus grounds, Chief Man-of-Bats and Batwing removed Professor Pyg's masks from the circus workers' faces.

Chief Man-of-Bats checked each person for injuries.

Once the circus workers were all cleared, Batwing returned all of the stolen goods.

Moments later, the Gotham City Police arrived at the scene. Police Commissioner James Gordon thanked the heroes for their help.

"The Circus of Strange is now out of business," Batman told him.

"And a perfect pen for Pyg is Arkham Asylum," Gordon said.

Gotham City was safe once again, thanks to Batman and his team of international heroes.

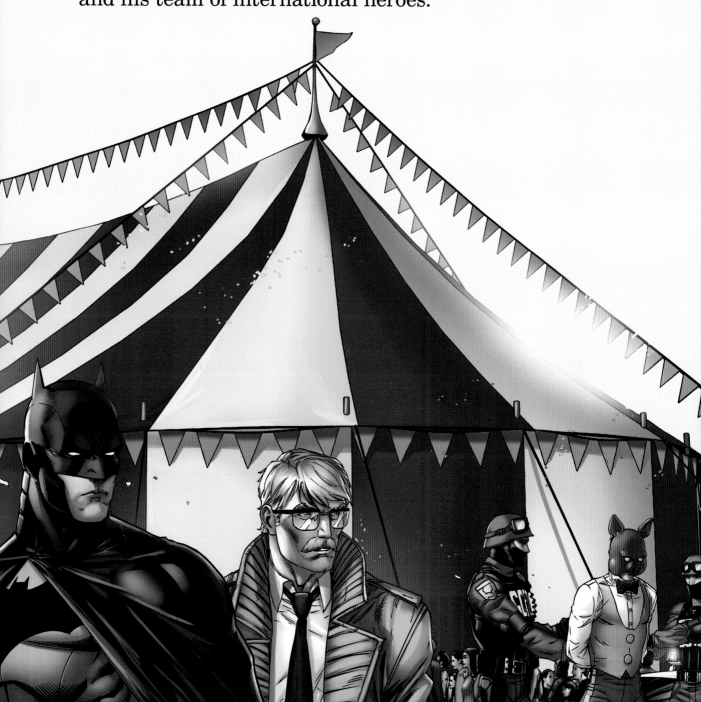

BATMAN

HARLEY QUINN'S PERFECT PRANK

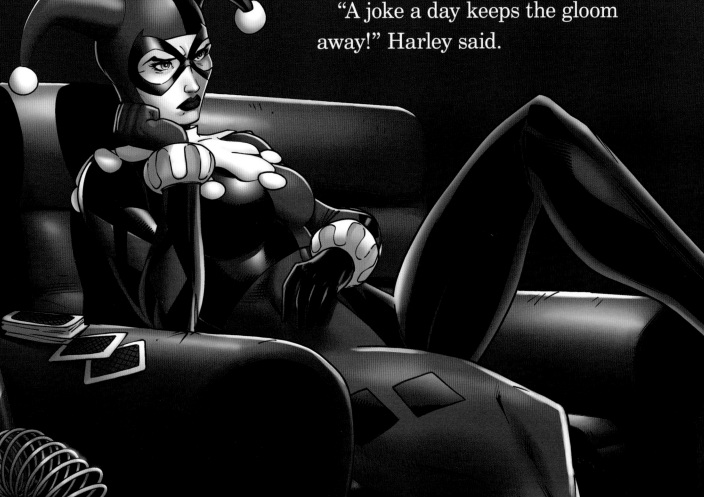

Inside her secret hideout, the villain Harley Quinn slumped in a chair. Ever since the Joker, her partner in crime, had been locked up in Arkham Asylum, she had been missing out on the action. She decided it was time for a crime spree.

"A joke a day keeps the gloom away!" Harley said.

First, Harley needed to find some new partners in crime. She called her friends Catwoman and Poison Ivy.

"Let's loot every shop in Gotham City!" she said.

"Sounds *purr*fect," Catwoman replied.

"Simply divine!" Poison Ivy agreed.

The trio climbed into Harley's clown car and tore through the streets of Gotham City.

When they reached downtown Gotham City,
the thieves split up. Catwoman stole diamonds, rubies,
and other priceless gems from a famous jewelry store.
Poison Ivy hit the Gotham City Museum of Art and stole
several masterpieces.

Harley Quinn snatched a ton of sweets and treats from
her favorite snack shop. "I feel like a kid in a candy store!"
she said with an evil laugh.

At Wayne Manor, billionaire Bruce Wayne was in his study with his son Damian. Suddenly, the Bat-Signal lit up the sky.

"Look, there is trouble in the city!" Damian said.

"To the Batcave!" Bruce replied.

Bruce and Damian rushed into a passageway that led deep below Wayne Manor to Bruce's secret hideout. The Batcave contained the uniforms, gadgets, and weapons of their secret identities, Batman and Robin—
the Dynamic Duo!

Batman and Robin hopped inside the Batmobile and zoomed out of the Batcave, headed toward Gotham City. The heroes quickly spotted Harley Quinn and her gang speeding away from the scenes of their crimes.

"Look!" said Catwoman, spotting the Batmobile gaining on them. "It's the bat!"

"And the brat!" added Poison Ivy.

Harley let out a laugh. "If they want to play," she said, "we'll play!"

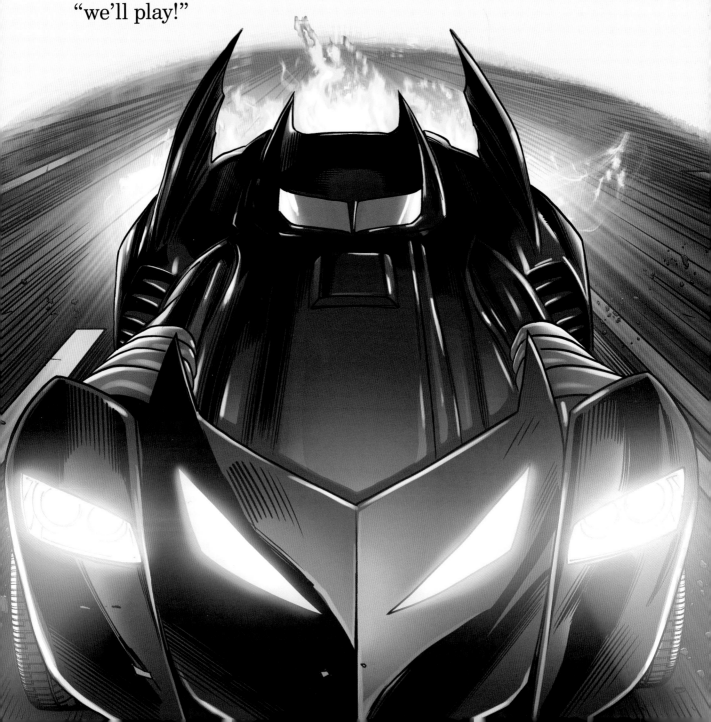

Harley Quinn pulled a lever on the dash of her car. "This old gag is a real hit!" she joked.

Suddenly, a huge boxing glove sprang out of the clown car's trunk. The glove punched the Batmobile, making it swerve and crash into a Dumpster.

The heroes climbed out of the mess. "They're going to get away!" shouted Robin.

"I don't think so," the Dark Knight said.

Batman quickly found another way to follow the thieves. He and Robin blasted into the air with rocket-powered jet packs. "I've got a few tricks of my own," said Batman.

In the chaos of the crash, Harley and her friends headed to the Gotham City Library. There, Harley found a priceless joke book. "I'll be checking this book out . . . forever!" she shouted.

But someone was watching the crooks from the shadows. It was Barbara Gordon. She was Police Commissioner Gordon's daughter.

Barbara quickly entered an empty storage room and changed into her secret identity—Batgirl. Then she followed the criminals through the dark night.

Soon, Harley Quinn, Catwoman, and Poison Ivy arrived at their new hideout. It was Ivy's greenhouse. "Let's put down roots over here," she said.

Inside, the three thieves threw a party to celebrate the success of their crime spree.

"A life of crime sure is sweet!" said Harley. The day's haul and her newfound partners in crime had cheered her spirits.

"Yes," echoed Catwoman.

"Talk about teamwork!"

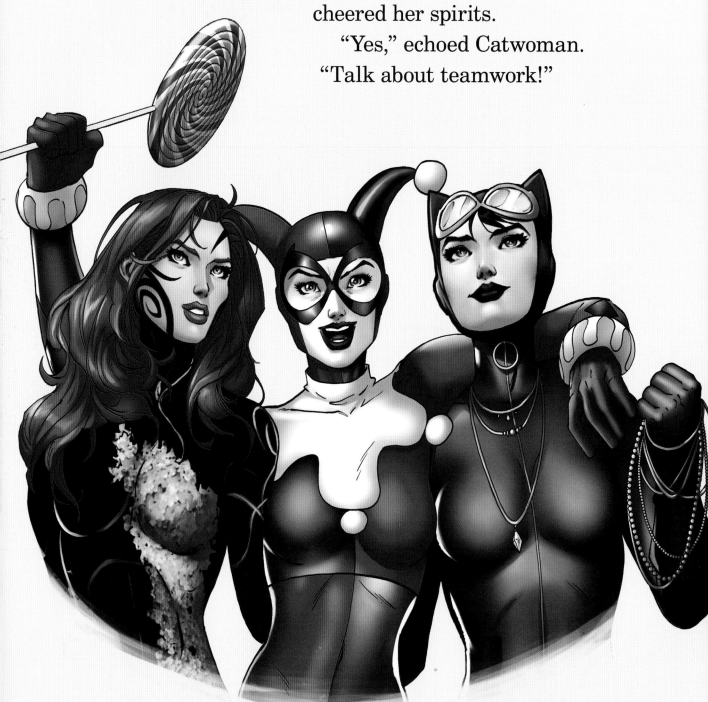

Suddenly, the Dynamic Duo crashed into the greenhouse with their jet packs.

"Hey!" Harley Quinn shouted. "This is a private party."

"Yeah, no bats or birds allowed!" added Poison Ivy.

Poison Ivy commanded her pet Venus flytrap to attack. It wrapped its thorny vines tightly around the heroes. The monstrous plant lifted Batman and Robin into the air. They dangled over its sharp, slimy teeth.

"Looks like you two are all tied up!" joked Harley.

Poison Ivy moved the heroes toward the plant's snapping jaws. "And soon to be plant food!" she shouted.

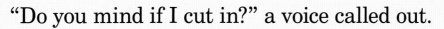
"Do you mind if I cut in?" a voice called out.
The villains turned to find Batgirl in the greenhouse
doorway atop her Batcycle. She hurled her Batarangs
at the Dynamic Duo. Their razor-sharp edges sliced
through the vines, freeing the two heroes.

The villains tried to escape, but Batman,
Robin, and Batgirl quickly swung their Batropes.
"Look who's tied up now!" said Robin.
"I guess the joke's on us," Harley
Quinn fumed.

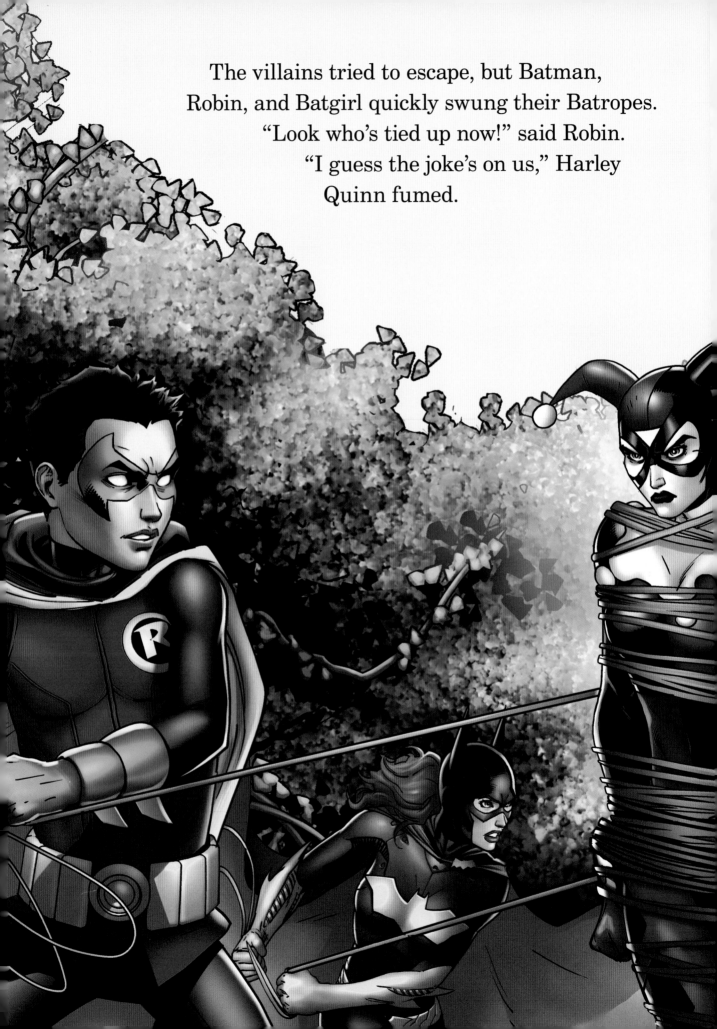

Moments later, the
Gotham City Police arrived.
Police Commissioner
James Gordon thanked
the heroes.
"You saved the day
again!" he said.

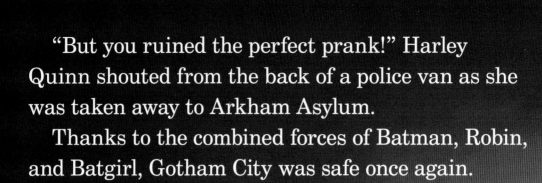

"But you ruined the perfect prank!" Harley Quinn shouted from the back of a police van as she was taken away to Arkham Asylum.

Thanks to the combined forces of Batman, Robin, and Batgirl, Gotham City was safe once again.

BATMAN™

THE TOMB OF ETERNAL LIFE

One evening, billionaire Bruce Wayne and his friend Dick Grayson attended a charity benefit at the Gotham City Museum. A legendary document was on display.

The glamorous heiress Kate Kane was also present. The three socialites gathered around the museum's main attraction.

"The Scroll of Osiris," Bruce said. "It is the oldest Egyptian document ever found. Some say it contains ancient secrets of immortality."

Suddenly, the glass skylight above them shattered
as a group of warriors dropped in on the startled crowd.
Bruce, Dick, and Kate slipped out the back door, while
the intruders surrounded the other guests.

A man emerged from the crowd. He was dressed in fine clothes and adorned with gold. "I am Rā's al Ghūl," he said. "I hope you have enjoyed yourselves, for the party is now over."

Rā's walked up to the display case and smashed the glass. Then he removed the priceless parchment.

Before Rā's could make his escape, the doors crashed open. Batman, Nightwing, and Batwoman rushed at the thieves, but the henchmen hurled exploding gas pellets. The super heroes were overcome by the fumes.

When the smoke cleared, Rā's and his men were gone.

Batman pulled out his mobile Batcomputer. Nightwing and Batwoman gathered around as the World's Greatest Detective investigated the theft.

"Why would Rā's steal the Scroll of Osiris?" Nightwing asked.

"Osiris was the Egyptian god of the Underworld," Batwoman said. "He could grant life after death. Many have performed magic rituals in his honor, in hopes of achieving eternal life."

"The scroll is really a map that leads to a ritual site," Batman said. "I believe it's also the location of a new Lazarus Pit."

"What's that?" asked Batwoman.

Nightwing explained how the liquid in these mystical pools had unknown restorative qualities.

"We must stop Rā's before he rejuvenates himself," Batman said. "The stronger he becomes, the harder he is to defeat."

Batman, Nightwing, and Batwoman went to the Batplane. The tracking device placed on the scroll by the museum showed that Rā's was headed for the Canyon of Tombs, a hidden sanctuary in Egypt.

The heroes flew for hours. Finally, the Canyon of Tombs appeared on the radar screen.

Batman landed the Batplane in a patch of desert. The three detectives trekked through the heat to the cave's underground entrance.

When the heroes entered the cave, Rā's al Ghūl's henchmen immediately surrounded them. The League of Assassins had seen them coming and were prepared for a fight. But they were no match for this terrific trio. Batman, Nightwing, and Batwoman quickly defeated the villains.

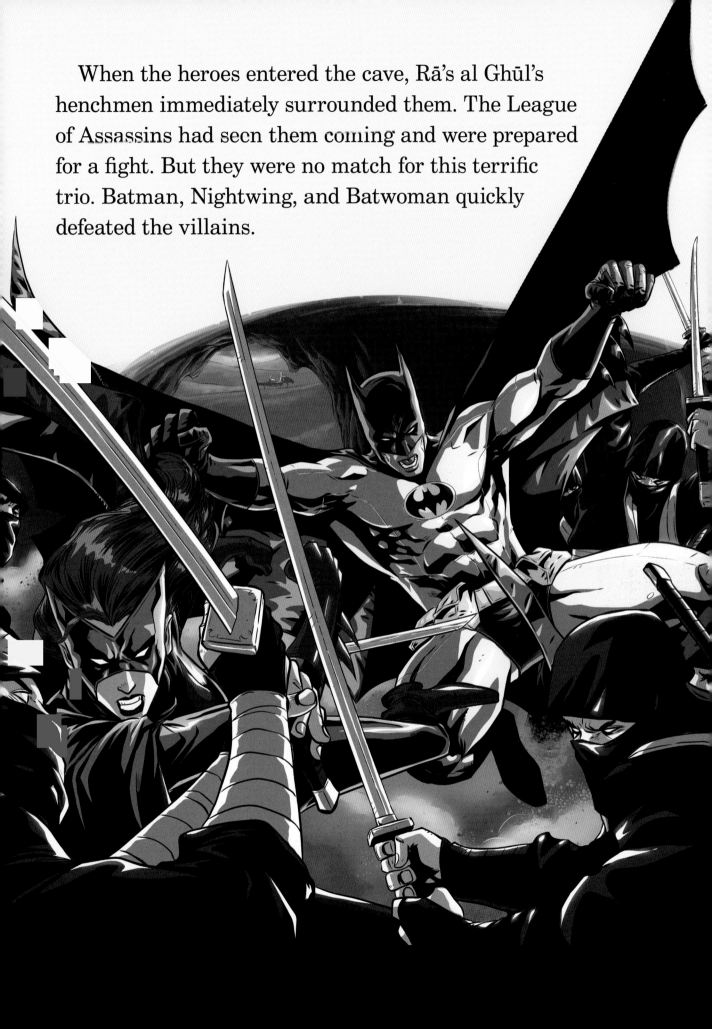

Deep inside the cave, Rā's al Ghūl was with his daughter, Talia, and their bodyguard, Ubu. They had discovered the new Lazarus Pit. Rā's was preparing to enter its rejuvenating waters.

"This bath contains infinite knowledge and helps grant eternal life," Rā's said. "Soon, I shall be revitalized!"

"Bath time is over," boomed a deep voice. It was Batman.

The Caped Crusader fired his grappling hook, ensnaring the villain, and pulled him away from the pit. Batwoman and Nightwing charged at Talia and Ubu.

"Eliminate them!" Rā's commanded as he pulled at the wires that bound him.

"You have great skill," Talia said as she battled with Batwoman. "Perhaps we will recruit you for the League."

"I've seen them in action," Batwoman replied. She knocked Talia down with a swift kick. "I'm not impressed."

Ubu rushed at Nightwing, trying to pulverize him with his fists, but the young hero was too quick. He expertly somersaulted over a stone altar and landed on Ubu's back, grabbing him in a headlock. "The bigger they are, the more fun they are to fight!" Nightwing exclaimed.

Rā's al Ghūl was able to loosen his binds enough to unsheathe his sword, the Serpent's Head. He sliced through the Batrope and lunged at the Dark Knight. "For this indignity, I will make you suffer!" he yelled.

"The League and I will cleanse the planet and start fresh," Rā's said as they battled. "This poor defiled world must be restored to its former glory!"

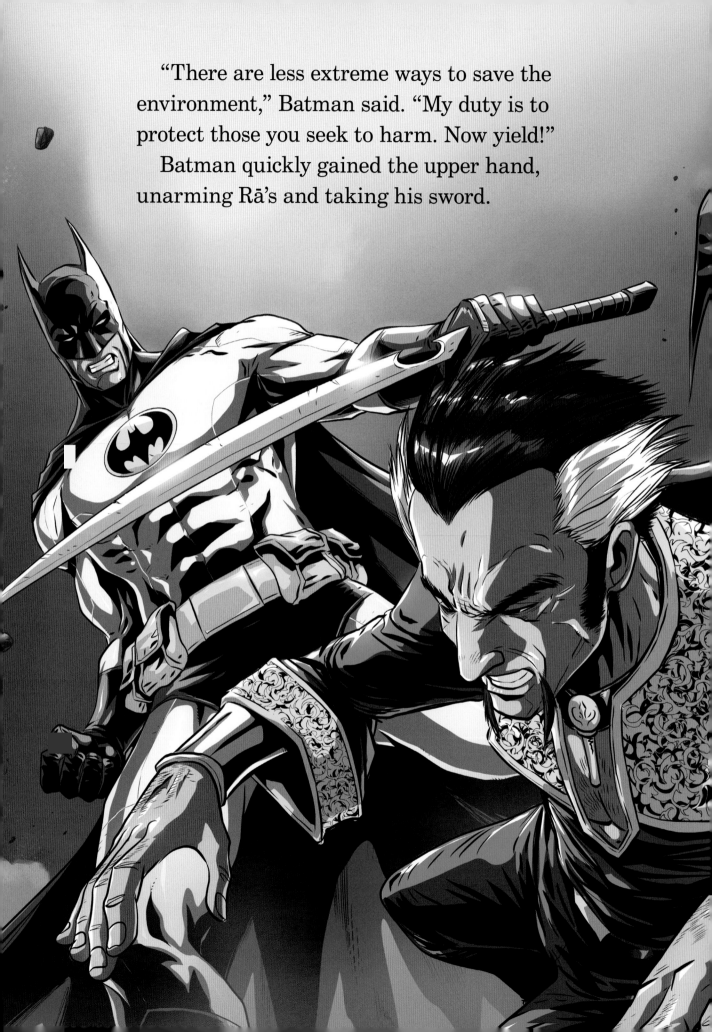

"There are less extreme ways to save the environment," Batman said. "My duty is to protect those you seek to harm. Now yield!" Batman quickly gained the upper hand, unarming Rā's and taking his sword.

Suddenly, the cavern walls began to tremble. The ground shook beneath their boots.

"We need to get out of here!" Batman shouted. The fighting had caused the fragile tomb walls to crack. They were starting to collapse!

Batman grabbed the Scroll of Osiris and put it in his Utility Belt.

Then he joined Nightwing, Batwoman, Talia, Ubu, and Rā's as they raced up the crumbling stairs. The stones gave way under their feet.

Seconds before the walkway disappeared, Batman, Nightwing, Batwoman, Talia, and Ubu made it to the surface. Rā's tumbled back, but Batman caught his hand. The villain dangled over the gaping chasm.

"Help me save you!" Batman grunted.

"Don't worry—this is only the beginning," Rā's al Ghūl replied calmly. "We shall meet again, Detective. . . ."

Rā's released Batman's hand and fell into the Lazarus Pit far below.

Nightwing and Batwoman handcuffed
Talia and Ubu and escorted them silently
to the Batplane.

Batman stared down into the pit. They'd
been so close to getting everyone out alive.

"You may have scattered the League, but this is a minor setback," Talia told the heroes. "We shall return with a vengeance. The League of Assassins will rise again!"

"And we will be ready to take you down *again*," Batman replied.

The Batplane took off, on its course back to Gotham City.

THE PENGUIN'S BIRDS OF PREY

Crime in Gotham City was at an all-time high. Citizens all over had had valuable possessions stolen from their homes. Each crime had turned up a single, odd clue: a bird's feather. Batman lurked at the scene of the latest robbery. He pocketed the feather and headed back to his secret hideout.

The Batcave was located deep below Wayne Manor. There, Batman analyzed all of the feathers he had collected from the various crime scenes.

"Master Bruce, this may be of interest to you," Alfred interrupted him. The butler pointed to a news report on the Batcomputer.

"Gotham City's birds have not returned from their migrations," said Beverly Birdsong, an environmentalist. "This is not natural. Something is wrong."

"Hmm. I bet these events are connected somehow," Batman said.

BYE BYE BIRD

Suddenly, an alarm sounded above them in Wayne Manor. Bruce and Alfred raced up to the study just in time to see a vulture fly out of a broken window. In its talons, it carried an upside-down umbrella containing Bruce Wayne's expensive gold watch, cell phone, and laptop.

"Must I remind you not to leave your toys lying around?" Alfred said.

"Don't worry, old friend," Bruce replied. "All of those items have tracking devices. The latest in Wayne Enterprises technology."

Alfred nodded. "And they'll lead us straight to the mastermind behind this caper."

Bruce hurried back to the Batcave to change into his Batsuit.

Batman followed the tracking signals through Gotham City's streets to the Iceberg Lounge. The lounge was a nightclub owned by the gangster Oswald Cobblepot. Several birds flew in through a skylight. Each one carried an umbrella.

The Caped Crusader landed the Batplane on a nearby roof. Then he followed the birds inside.

Batman found himself in Oswald Cobblepot's private office. The gangster hopped up to greet the Caped Crusader. "I'll have you know, this is an exclusive club," he said. "Not all flying creatures are welcome."

"Mr. Cobblepot, I presume?" Batman asked. "So you're the one behind all this fowl play."

"Yes," squawked Oswald. "But you can call me the Penguin!"

"What's your game, Penguin?" the hero said.

The villain narrowed his beady eyes and smiled. "My feathered friends are helping me become the richest man in Gotham City. Soon I'll move into Wayne Manor and kick Bruce Wayne to the curb!"

"The only big house you'll be going to is Blackgate Penitentiary," said Batman.

The Penguin blew on a whistle, commanding the birds' attention. In an instant, birds of all feathers descended on Batman. They pecked and scratched and clawed at the Caped Crusader.

"I've spent all winter hypnotizing these wonderful creatures to do my bidding," the gangster explained. "Now I'll have them rid me of my rodent infestation once and for all!"

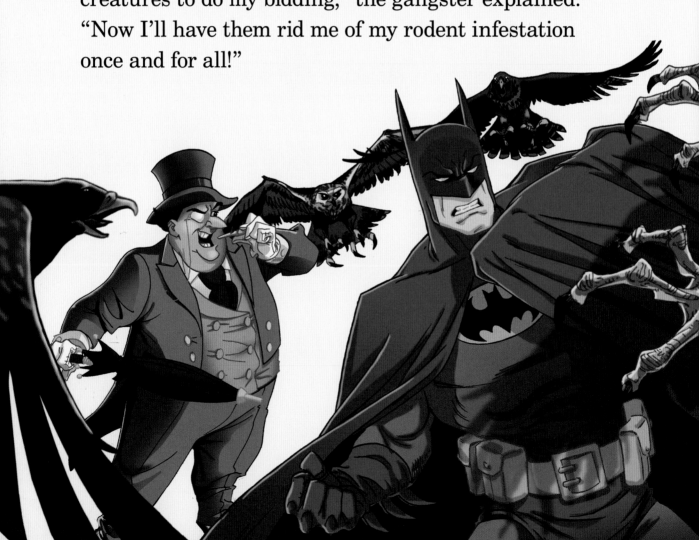

Batman quickly hurled a Batarang at the sprinkler system, releasing a torrent of water. The birds snapped out of their trance and flew out of the skylight.

"Curses!" hollered the Penguin.

"Those birds needed a break, and so do you!" Batman said.

He tackled the Penguin, and they crashed through the office door into the lounge.

As they hit the ground, the villain whipped out his trick umbrella. He pointed the end at Batman and sprayed him with a cloud of gas. *Fwhoosh!* The hero coughed and sputtered, trying to catch his breath.

The Penguin's wicked weapon transformed into an umbrella jet pack! It lifted him up over the ballroom toward another skylight in the ceiling.

"Penguins do not fly unless it is with style!" the villain called as he made his escape.

"Time to put this turkey on ice," Batman growled.
He reached into his Utility Belt and pulled out
a freeze bomb. He hurled the device at the fancy
fountain down below.

The bomb exploded when it hit the statue. The giant seal sculpture erupted and a wave of water washed over the Penguin, who was flying overhead. The chemicals within the bomb froze the water in the fountain, instantly trapping the villain.

Minutes later, the Gotham City Police arrived. Batman filled Commissioner Gordon in on the Penguin's crimes.

"He trained the birds to steal by flying in and out of homes," Batman said. "That's the reason you never found a culprit."

"Your help is much appreciated, Batman," said Commissioner Gordon.

"It was nothing," Batman replied. "I love a good mystery."

The Penguin was still trapped in his frozen prison. Two officers worked to break the ice. Then they transferred the Penguin to Blackgate Penitentiary, and the stolen valuables were returned to their rightful owners.

The next day, Bruce and Alfred went bird watching
with Beverly Birdsong. "I'm so glad these beautiful birds
are flying free!" she said as a vulture soared high above
the trees. "No bird should be in captivity!"

Alfred agreed, but Bruce was not so sure. "Oh, I can
think of *one* bird that belongs in a cage," Bruce said with
a smile. "The Penguin!"

BATMAN

THE JOKER'S NIGHT OF FRIGHT

In Gotham City, four costumed criminals met in a run-down building.

"The Fright Club is now in session!" said the Joker. He and Harley Quinn had recruited the Scarecrow and Mad Hatter for their latest caper.

"Together, we'll strike fear in the heart of Gotham City," the Scarecrow said.

"And strike down the Dynamic Duo!" added Mad Hatter. The Joker explained his evil plan to his partners in crime.

The next night, Batman and Robin were patrolling the city in the Batmobile when the Bat-Signal suddenly lit up the sky. But the usual symbol of a bat had been replaced by a smiling cat. The two heroes were confused.

"Is that a joke?" Robin asked.

"If it is, it's not funny," said Batman grimly. "Let's go investigate the scene."

The Dynamic Duo raced to Gotham City Police Headquarters.

When they reached the roof of the building, where the Bat-Signal was located, they were surprised by what they found. The culprit was Commissioner Gordon!

The commissioner was acting strangely. Robin removed his hat, and the commissioner snapped out of his trance.

"This mind-control device is the calling card of the Mad Hatter," Batman said.

Commissioner Gordon couldn't remember anything that had happened before the heroes arrived.

Batman found a sprig of straw on the ground. He scanned it with his goggles and discovered it was laced with the Scarecrow's fear toxin.

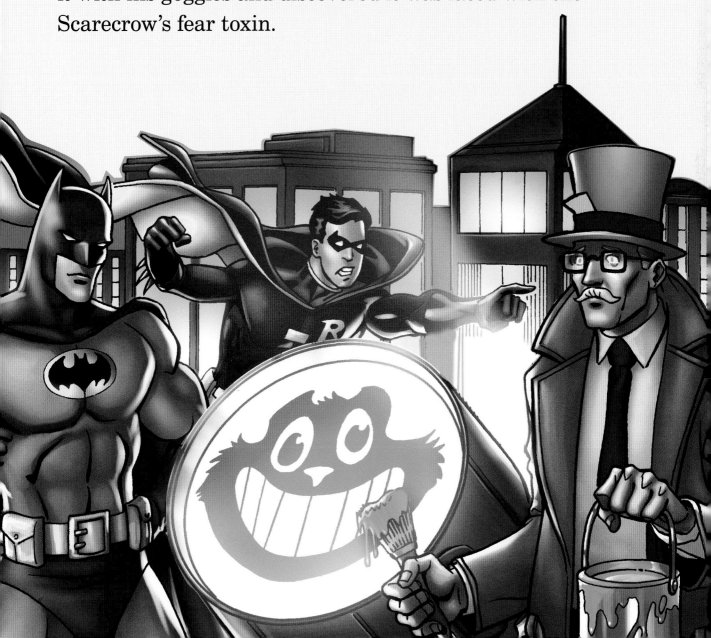

"Look!" Robin called out, pointing to the far wall.

Red paint dripped off the bricks. A message was signed with the grinning head of a court jester. It read, "Lost in a room of the house, disguised as a flying mouse, the bat is ready to pounce, but he will fall and bounce!"

"The Joker is up to his old tricks," Batman said. "The evidence shows he's joined forces with Mad Hatter and the Scarecrow."

"And this message is a clue to where they will strike," added the Boy Wonder.

"Luckily, I know exactly where that is," Batman replied. "To the Batmobile!"

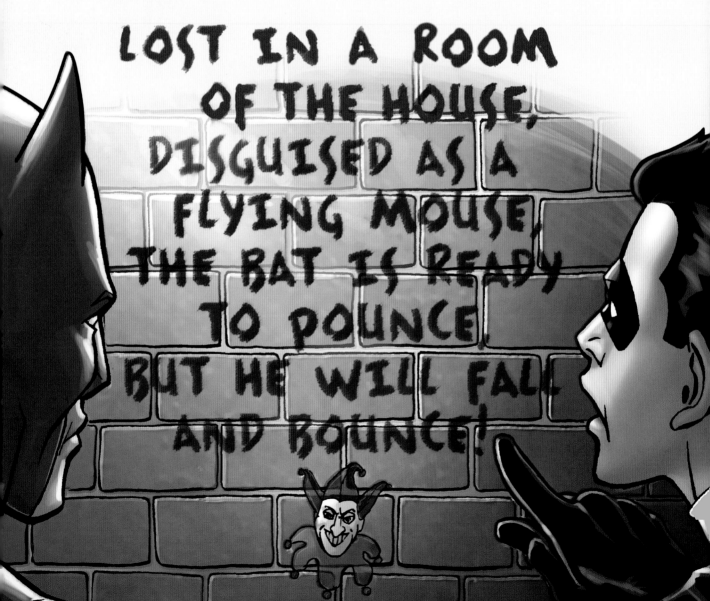

Batman and Robin leaped down to their waiting vehicle.

"How did you solve that riddle?" Robin asked.

"Quite simply," Batman stated. "The phrases 'room of the house,' 'disguised as,' and 'fall and bounce' describe the words 'hall,' 'costume,' and 'ball.'"

Robin's face lit up. "Of course . . . the biggest party in Gotham City," he replied. "It's happening right now."

Across town, Mayor Sebastian Hady greeted his guests at the City Hall Costume Ball. He was dressed as Zeus, a Greek god. The other partygoers were bedecked in costumes, masks, and jewels as well.

Suddenly, the doors crashed open. The Joker stepped into the room, followed by Scarecrow, Mad Hatter, and Harley Quinn. "We're here to collect for my Hilarity Charity!" yelled the Joker. "That means we're stealing your cash and laughing all the way to the bank! HA-HA-HA!"

The Scarecrow sprayed the room with his fear toxin. The guests suffered from the effects of the toxin while the criminals stole their valuables.

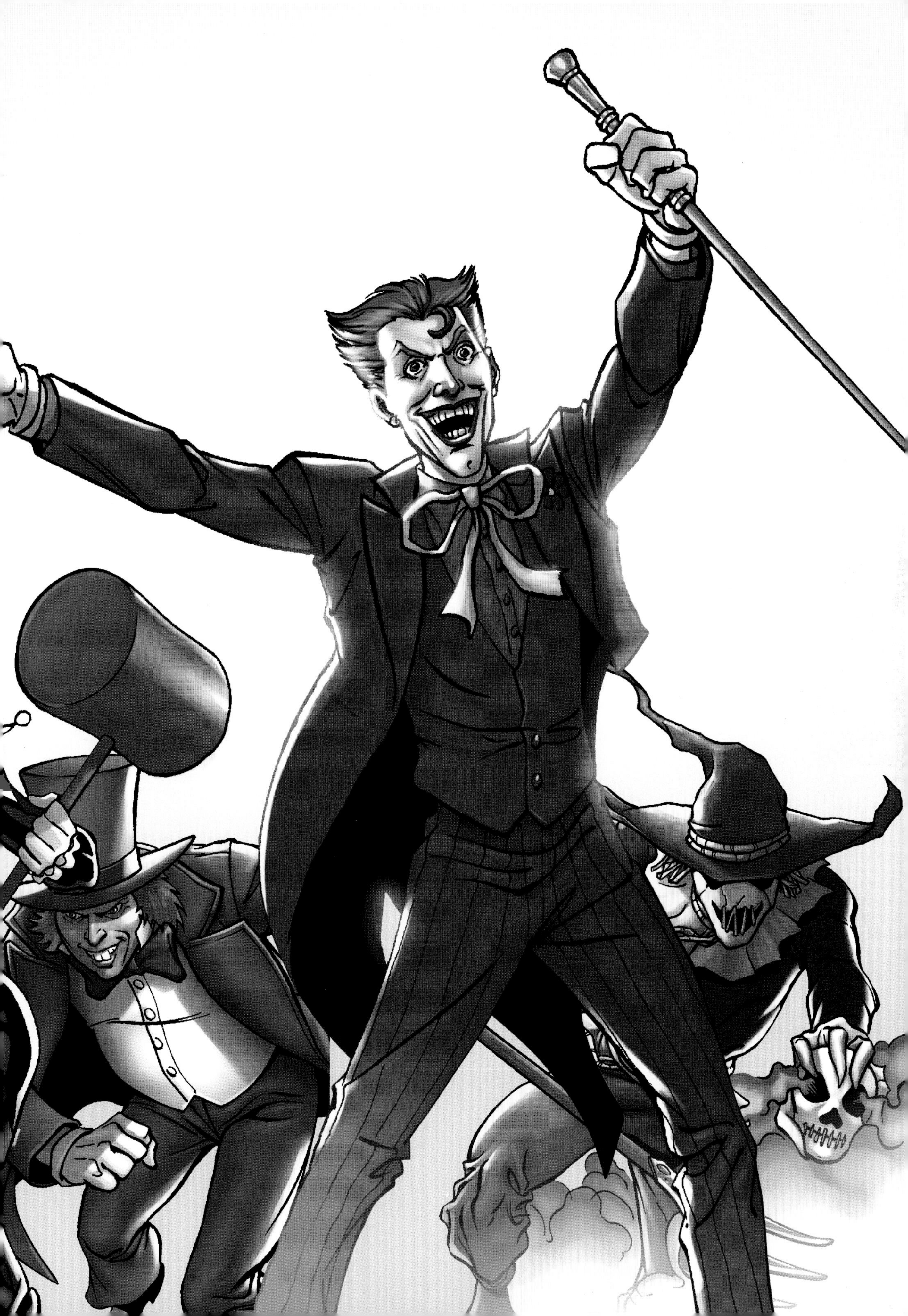

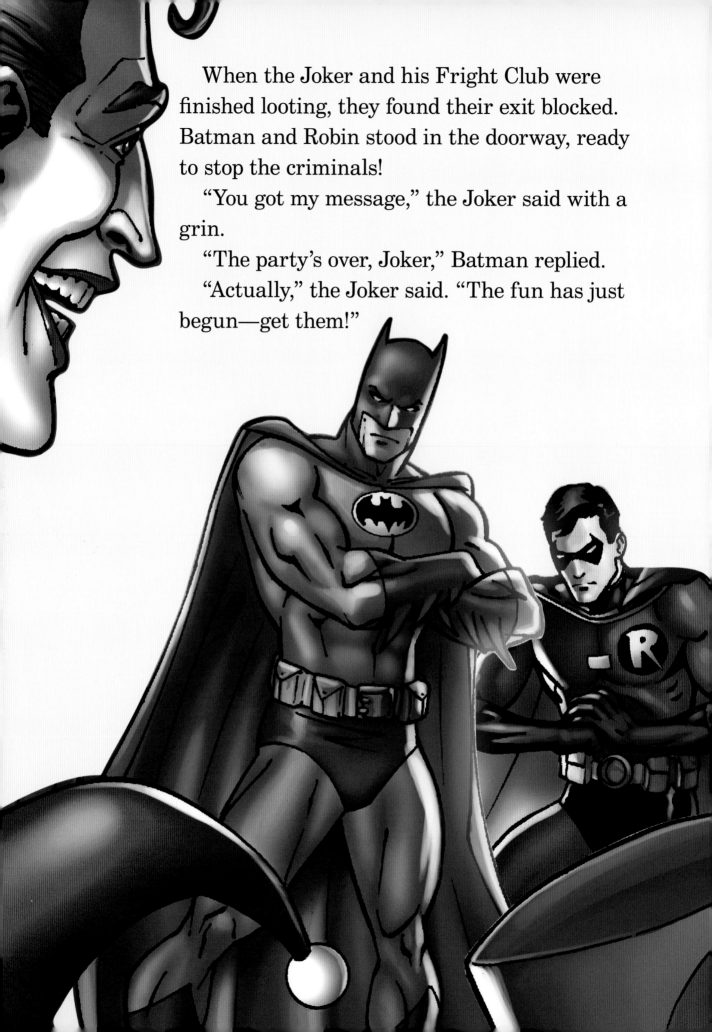

When the Joker and his Fright Club were finished looting, they found their exit blocked. Batman and Robin stood in the doorway, ready to stop the criminals!

"You got my message," the Joker said with a grin.

"The party's over, Joker," Batman replied.

"Actually," the Joker said. "The fun has just begun—get them!"

The Scarecrow grabbed his poison blaster, and the Joker pointed his deadly flower at Batman. They fired at the Caped Crusader together. Batman ducked just in time, and the villains sprayed each other.

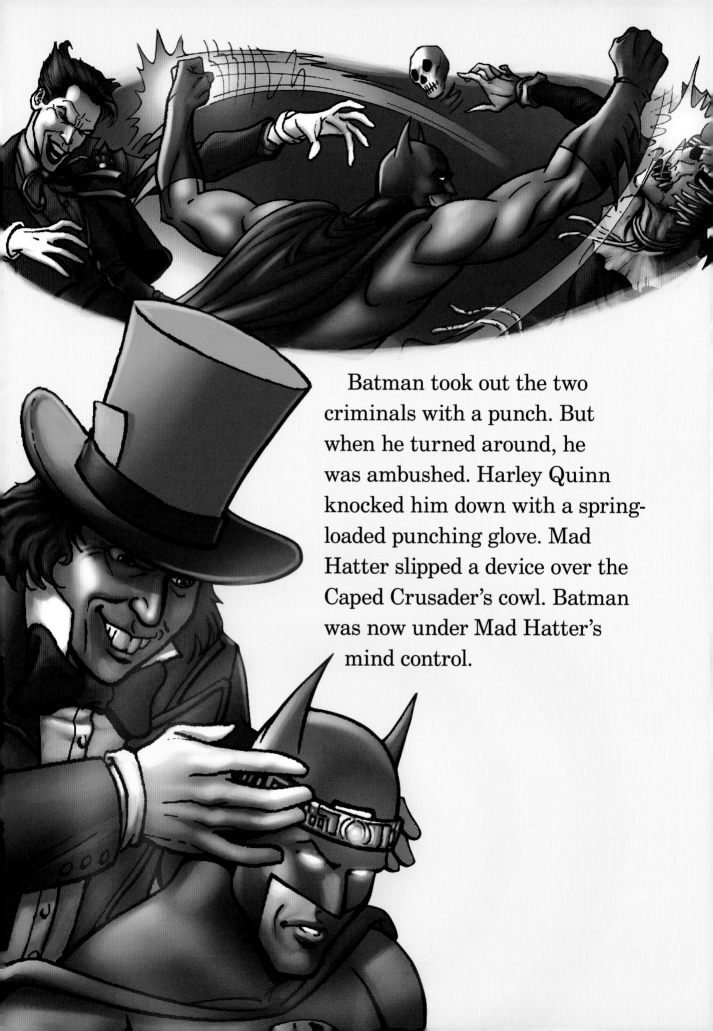

Batman took out the two criminals with a punch. But when he turned around, he was ambushed. Harley Quinn knocked him down with a spring-loaded punching glove. Mad Hatter slipped a device over the Caped Crusader's cowl. Batman was now under Mad Hatter's mind control.

"Do as I command, Batman," said Mad Hatter. "Dispose of Robin!"

Batman picked up his partner and headed for the open window. Robin struggled to break free, but Batman was too strong. "Let's see if this little birdie can fly!" yelled the Caped Crusader.

Robin grabbed a Batarang from his Utility Belt and hurled the weapon at Mad Hatter. The Batarang knocked out the villain, severing the mind-control link with Batman.

The hero put Robin down and pulled off the Mad Hatter's device. He crushed it in his hands.

"This ends now!" he yelled.

While Robin faced off against the Scarecrow, Harley Quinn seized the opportunity for a sneak attack.

"Robin, behind you!" Batman yelled.

The Boy Wonder grabbed the Scarecrow and threw the villain over his shoulder. Scarecrow flew into Harley Quinn, and both of the criminals crashed to the floor. Batman tied the two crooks together with his Batrope.

Seeing his plans falling apart, the Joker snatched all the loot he could and made a run for it.

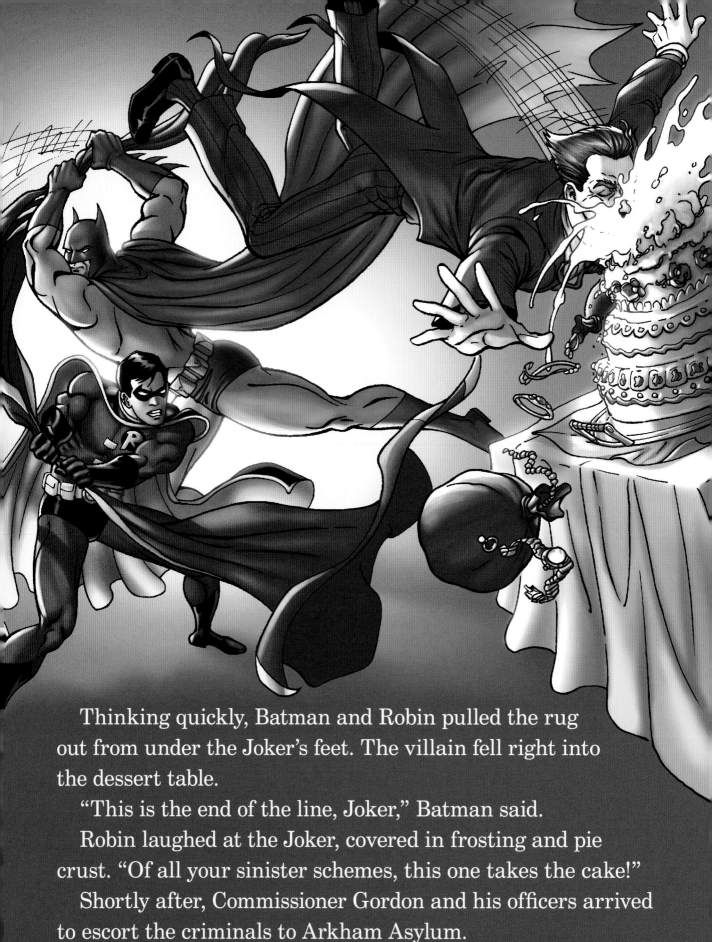

Thinking quickly, Batman and Robin pulled the rug out from under the Joker's feet. The villain fell right into the dessert table.

"This is the end of the line, Joker," Batman said.

Robin laughed at the Joker, covered in frosting and pie crust. "Of all your sinister schemes, this one takes the cake!"

Shortly after, Commissioner Gordon and his officers arrived to escort the criminals to Arkham Asylum.

"Thanks to you, the Fright Club is now out of business," the commissioner told the heroes.

Mayor Hady walked over with a gold trophy. "Not only did Batman and Robin save the day," he said, "but they won first prize for best costumes!"

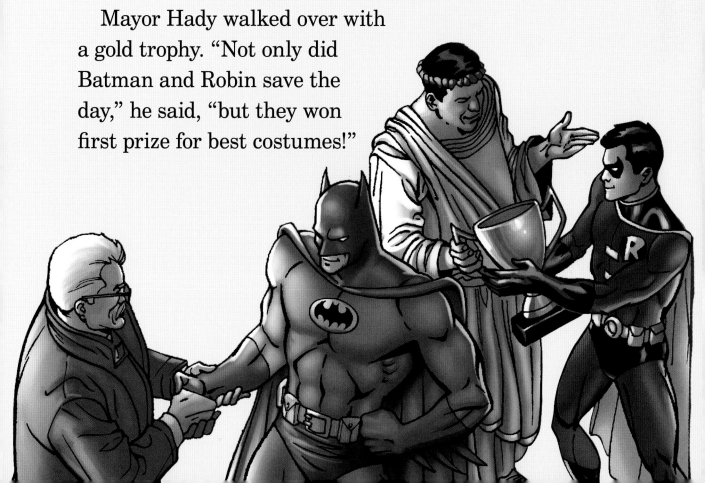

Batman and Robin thanked the commissioner and the mayor. Then they zipped off into the night on their Batropes. There were more crimes to solve and citizens to protect, as the Dynamic Duo fought to keep Gotham City safe.

BATMAN™

REPTILE REVENGE

Late one night, Batman and Robin, the Dynamic Duo, were working inside the Batcave. Suddenly, a breaking news story appeared on the high-tech Batcomputer. The reporter said that a famous doctor had been kidnapped.

"The doctor's whereabouts are unknown," the reporter said. "But police have reported signs of a struggle at his office."

Batman and Robin hopped into the Batmobile and drove across the city. Within moments, they arrived at the doctor's office. The Gotham City Police were already there, surveying the scene. Batman and Robin helped them investigate. The room had been slashed. Jagged claw marks covered the walls and the floors.

The evidence pointed to one criminal. "Killer Croc," the Caped Crusader told the police.

Batman reviewed the security tape from the doctor's office with Police Commissioner Gordon.

"Where is the antidote?" Croc yelled at the doctor.

"I don't have it here," the doctor told him. "It's at Gotham General Hospital."

The tape cut out. Commissioner Gordon turned to his officers. "Let's get to Gotham General and make sure it's clear," he said.

But Batman had a plan of his own.

Batman perched outside of Gotham General Hospital after the police swept through the building. As night fell over Gotham City, a dark figure snuck inside.

"This is too easy," Croc said as he stole the bottles of the antidote. But when he turned to leave, he found himself face-to-face with Batman.

"Do you have an appointment?" Batman asked.

"Batman," Croc growled. "Get out of my way."

Batman approached the raging reptile. "I can help you," the hero said. "Just come with me."

"The only person who can help me is *me*," Croc said. He charged at the Dark Knight. Croc was strong, but Batman was fast. The Dark Knight moved out of the way, and Croc crashed through the window.

Croc landed safely on the street below. He looked back up at Batman and smiled. Then he disappeared into the sewers.

When Commissioner Gordon heard what had happened, he was furious. "You let him get away!" shouted Gordon.

"No, I didn't," replied Batman calmly. The Caped Crusader held up a small screen showing a flashing red dot. "He'll take us right to the doctor," the super hero said.

Batman had placed a tracking device on Croc's scaly skin when the criminal rushed by him to make his escape.

"How will you follow him in the sewers?" asked the commissioner.

"I can help with that," said a voice. Robin stood in the doorway. He held two high-tech scuba suits and masks.

Batman and Robin prepared to go after Croc. Once they were suited up, they swam through the sewers, following the red dot on the tracking device. Finally, the dot stopped moving. They had found Croc's hideout.

The Dynamic Duo saw the missing doctor tied up inside. "I'll untie the doc," Robin whispered. "You stop the Croc."

Croc was mixing the antidote he had stolen so he could cure himself of his crocodile traits.

"It ends now," Batman said, surprising the villain.

Croc whirled around. "Batman!" Croc growled. "You're just in time for dinner. My pets are very hungry!"

Batman turned to see two crocodiles climbing up out of the sewer water.

The crocodiles were on top of Batman in an instant as Killer Croc made his getaway. The super hero struggled against their chomping jaws and razor-sharp teeth, but he couldn't hold them for long.

Batman reached for the reptile repellent in his Utility Belt and sprayed the beasts. Their jaws relaxed, and they quickly fell asleep.

After defeating the crocodiles, Batman caught up to the super-villain.

"You can't beat me, Batman," Croc cried when he saw that the hero was advancing on him again.

"I'm here to help you," Batman said. "There are good doctors in prison."

"No one's ever helped me before. Why would they start now?" Croc yelled. He lunged at Batman.

The pair wrestled to the ground. Using his martial arts skills, Batman fought to keep himself out of Croc's jaws. He kicked and punched the hulking beast, but Croc was too strong to keep down.

Robin saw that Batman was in trouble. He quickly
grabbed the antidote Croc had stolen. "You want this,
Lizard Lips?" Robin shouted at the super-villain. "Come
and get it!"

He tossed the medication into the rushing flow of
sewer water.

"No!" Croc screamed. He dived in after the bottles.

Batman and Robin dived into the sewer after Croc. They caught him just before he reached the bottles.

The Dynamic Duo grabbed the hulking beast and held his arms. Croc twisted and twirled beneath the water, spinning the heroes like a washing machine. He was still too strong! Quickly realizing that they couldn't beat Croc with strength alone, Batman signaled to Robin that they needed to split up.

Killer Croc took off after Robin. He thought the Boy Wonder would be easier to catch. Then he could defeat Batman on his own. But the Boy Wonder had a plan. He swam into a narrow pipe.

Croc followed, but he was too big! He growled and gnashed his teeth, but he couldn't catch Robin now.

Robin climbed out the other side, but the big beast was stuck.

The police arrived and freed Croc from the sewer.

"Good work, Boy Wonder," Batman said. "That was one tight spot."

Then they took Croc away to where he could get the medical help he really needed.

BATMAN

THE JOKE'S ON WHO?

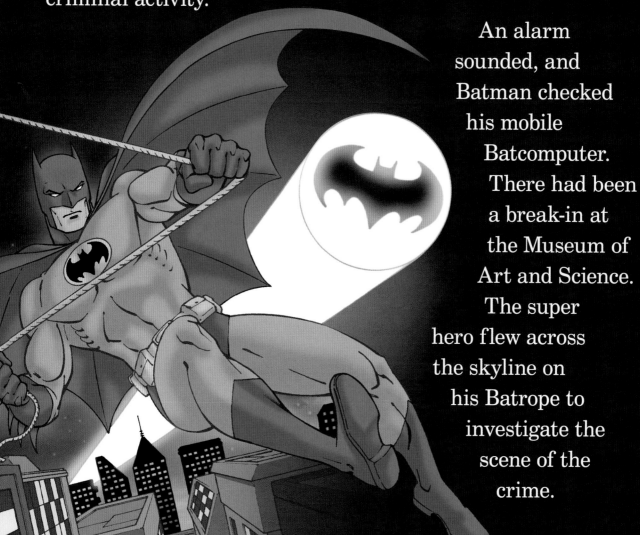

As night fell in Gotham City, Batman was on watch. He patrolled the rooftops and alleyways, on the lookout for any criminal activity.

An alarm sounded, and Batman checked his mobile Batcomputer. There had been a break-in at the Museum of Art and Science. The super hero flew across the skyline on his Batrope to investigate the scene of the crime.

The Caped Crusader landed on the museum roof and surveyed the scene. He spotted the Joker! The Clown Prince of Crime had stolen a priceless green pendant from the meteorite exhibit.

"You're too late, Batman!" the Joker yelled as he climbed into his blimp. "Come back during regular visiting hours! HA-HA!"

The villain took off, leaving Batman on the roof of the museum empty-handed.

"You won't be laughing for long, Joker," Batman growled.

Batman called the Batplane via remote control. "The Joker isn't the only one with an ace up his sleeve," the hero said as he got into his vehicle and zoomed after the blimp.

He used the plane's tracking device to follow the Joker. The criminal was headed to Metropolis, the home of one of Batman's fellow super heroes—Superman!

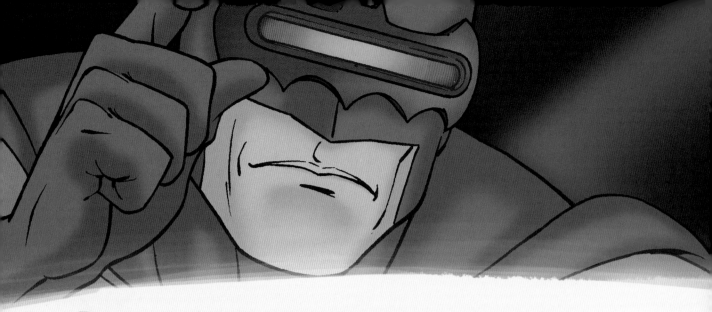

Batman trailed the Joker all the way to the LexCorp building. The Joker and Lex Luthor were having a private meeting. As he listened in, the Dark Knight learned that Luthor had hired the Joker to destroy the Man of Steel.

"This pendant is the key to Superman's undoing," Lex said, admiring the meteorite. "With him out of the way, Metropolis will be mine!"

"*Ours*," the Joker corrected the villain. "Don't forget, I'm doing all the dirty work."

Batman contacted Superman, and the two heroes met at the Daily Planet Building. "The Joker is very dangerous," Batman told the Man of Steel. "Beware of his next move."

"Likewise, Lex Luthor is crafty," Superman replied. "Let's team up to take them down."

Together, the world's finest heroes were ready for action!

The next day, Clark Kent was working at the Daily Planet with his co-worker Lois Lane. Jimmy Olsen, a photographer for the paper, ran into the newsroom. "You've got to see this!" he cried. "Hurry!"

Outside the window, the Joker's enormous blimp flew over the building. The Joker yelled into a bullhorn, "I am no longer a one-town clown. I'm taking my creep show on a world tour. HA-HA-HA!"

"Who is that?" Lois exclaimed.

But Clark was already a step ahead of his co-workers.

Clark slipped into a private closet and revealed his super hero uniform under his suit. "This looks like a job for Superman," he said.

Across town, Lex Luthor was having lunch at a popular rooftop restaurant when the Joker's blimp appeared in the sky. The criminal clown entered the dining area.

"I am joining you for lunch!" the Joker cried, pointing at Lex. "I'll order the bald billionaire, please . . . to go!" He quickly tied Lex up and dragged him toward the waiting blimp.

Suddenly, the Man of Steel appeared!

"Just my luck," the Joker sneered. "Everywhere I go there's a big blockhead in long pajamas."

"Your luck has run out," Superman said sternly.

The Joker approached Superman with his hands up. When he was close enough, he slipped the pendant around the hero's neck. "Here's a jewel for the flying fool!" the Joker giggled.

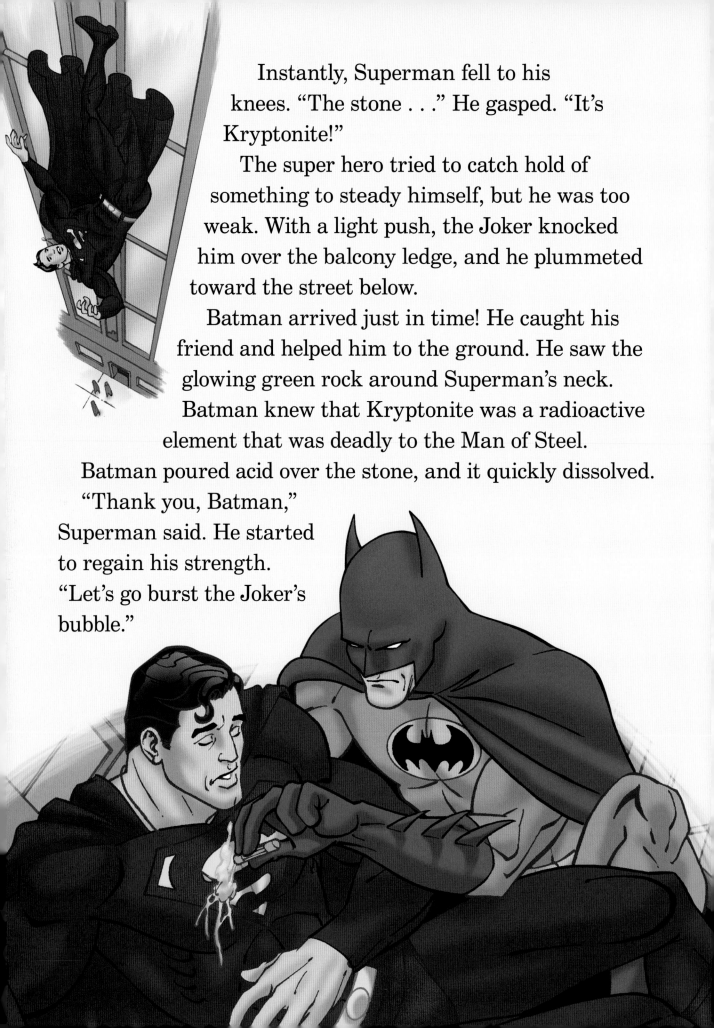

Instantly, Superman fell to his knees. "The stone . . ." He gasped. "It's Kryptonite!"

The super hero tried to catch hold of something to steady himself, but he was too weak. With a light push, the Joker knocked him over the balcony ledge, and he plummeted toward the street below.

Batman arrived just in time! He caught his friend and helped him to the ground. He saw the glowing green rock around Superman's neck. Batman knew that Kryptonite was a radioactive element that was deadly to the Man of Steel.

Batman poured acid over the stone, and it quickly dissolved.

"Thank you, Batman," Superman said. He started to regain his strength. "Let's go burst the Joker's bubble."

The Joker, with Lex Luthor as his prisoner, was flying his blimp all around Metropolis. "This big balloon is filled with my poisonous Joker Gas," he said. "It'll leave a smile on your face whether you like it or not. Hee-hee-hee!"

Luthor was furious. "This wasn't the plan," he yelled.

"Sharing is caring, Lex," the Joker replied. "And I don't care! With you and Superman out of the way, nothing can stop me."

Suddenly, Superman and Batman smashed through the wall of the blimp.

"Guess again, Joker!" Superman exclaimed. "You're not the only one with a powerful partner."

"Another uninvited pest!" the Joker yelled when he saw Batman. "Go haunt a house, you flying mouse!"

"Party's over," Batman said.

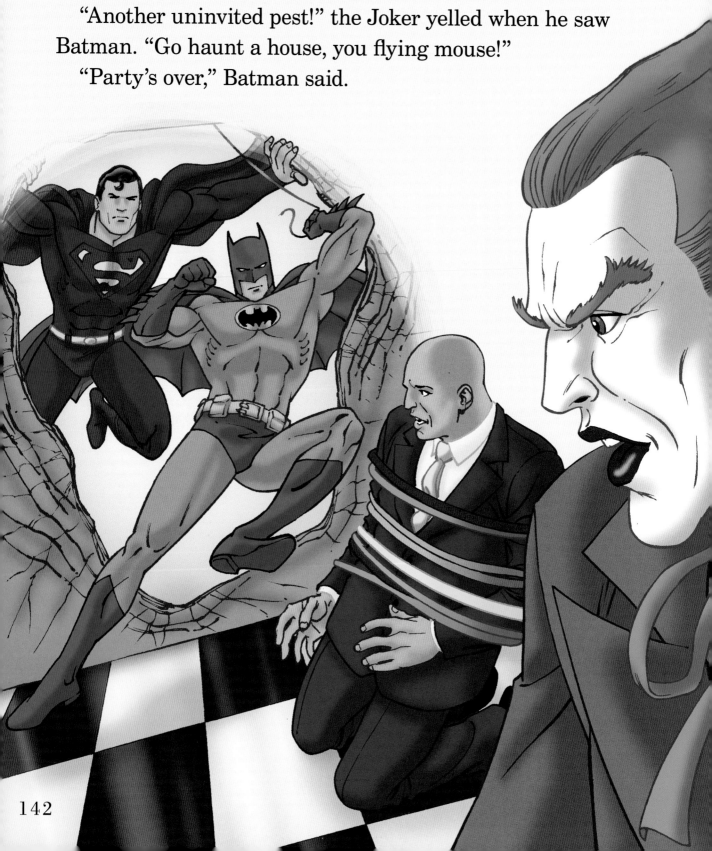

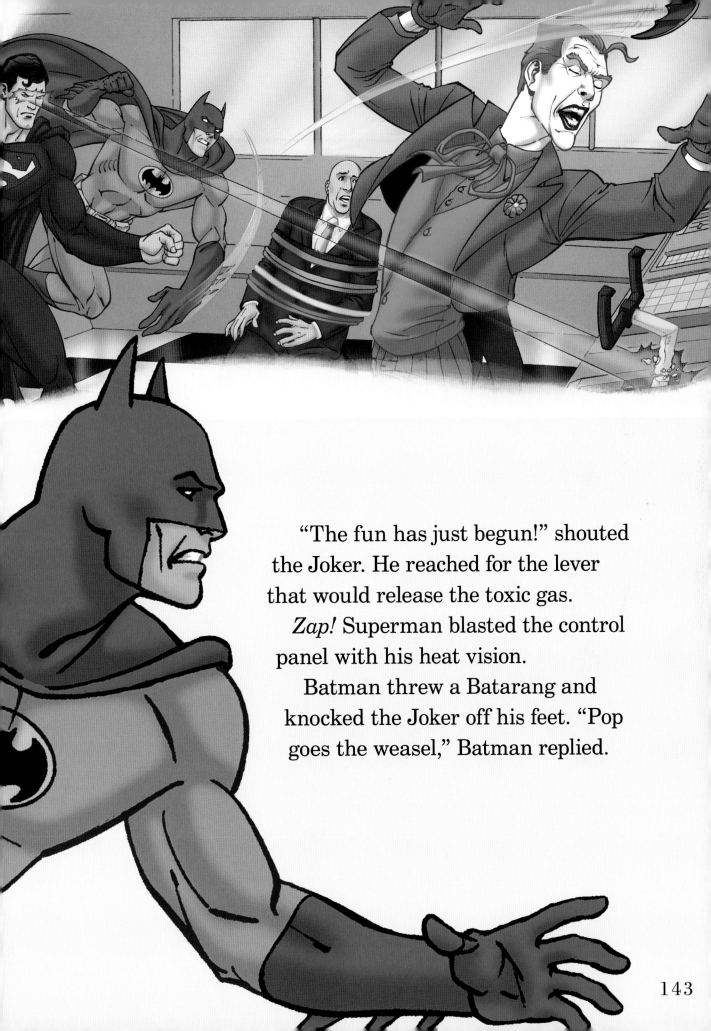

"The fun has just begun!" shouted the Joker. He reached for the lever that would release the toxic gas.

Zap! Superman blasted the control panel with his heat vision.

Batman threw a Batarang and knocked the Joker off his feet. "Pop goes the weasel," Batman replied.

Superman used his super-strength to push the blimp toward the nearest skyscraper. It was the Daily Planet Building. He carried Lex Luthor and the Joker down to the roof, with Batman close behind. Lois and Jimmy were there to cover the story.

The Metropolis police arrived and arrested the criminals.

Batman turned to Superman. "I'd better get back to Gotham," he said.

"Gotham City is lucky to have a hero like you," Superman said as he shook Batman's hand.

"We're lucky to have both of you," said Lois Lane.

"Yes," added Jimmy, "what a terrific team!" He snapped a few photos of the heroes for the next day's front-page story.

BATMAN

BATMAN AND THE TOXIC TERROR

As the sun rose in Gotham City, billionaire Bruce Wayne woke up inside Wayne Manor. He got out of bed, threw on a robe, and walked into his nearby study. His loyal butler, Alfred Pennyworth, was already there, pouring Bruce his morning cup of coffee.

Bruce turned on his flat-screen TV and changed the channel to the local news.

"Happy Earth Day, Gotham City," Claire Cameron, a perky newscaster, chirped on-screen. "I'm coming to you live from Harris Park. Today this piece of nature will be bulldozed to make way for a brand-new shopping mall."

Bruce couldn't believe it! The park was a city treasure.

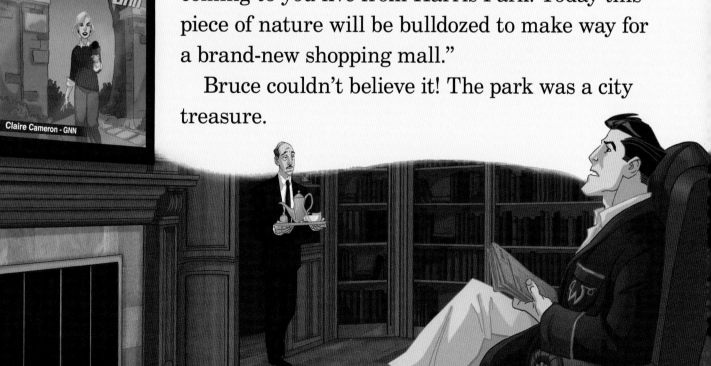

Claire Cameron - GNN

Bruce wasn't the only one who was upset by what was happening. The super-villain Poison Ivy was watching the bulldozers and camera crews.

"My park! My festival of foliage! What are those people doing?" she screamed. "If Gotham City's politicians have their way, soon every square block will be a slab of concrete. I have to stop them!"

Poison Ivy leaped from the tree and began planning her attack.

Claire Cameron - GNN

Back at Wayne Manor, Bruce called all of his wealthy friends and business partners and every government official he knew.

"Why is precious green space being sacrificed for yet another mall?" Bruce asked the mayor. "Some of these trees are hundreds of years old!"

Suddenly, a breaking news report on the television interrupted Bruce's phone call. He turned his attention back to the screen.

"We interrupt our regularly scheduled programming to bring you this breaking story. In a mysterious turn of Earth Day events," the reporter stated, "people here are turning into trees!"

Bruce and Alfred watched in horror as innocent Gotham citizens standing in the park found their legs rooted into the ground like tree trunks. Their arms turned stiff as branches. Bruce turned off the television.

"There's only one person capable of this," he said to Alfred. "Poison Ivy!"

Bruce raced to his secret hideout, hidden deep below Wayne Manor. Inside the Batcave, Bruce changed into his alter ego, Batman. His suit, weapons, and vehicles stood ready to help him fight the city's criminals.

In Harris Park, Poison Ivy was on a rampage. She sprayed a toxin at everyone she came across. She was turning the people into an army of trees!

Batman zoomed into downtown Gotham City on
the Batcycle, passing dozens of people who had been
transformed. Block after city block, they stood frozen in
conversation, checking their watches, sipping their coffee.
They looked exactly like they would have any other day—
except they were trees!

Pulling to a screeching halt at Harris
Park, Batman found two scared park
rangers huddled outside the gates.
"She ran that way," the taller one
yelled, pointing.

Following the ranger's tip, Batman entered the park. He used his razor-sharp Batarang to tear through the thickets and tangled vines before him. In only a few short hours, Poison Ivy had turned a friendly park into an impenetrable jungle.

From high above, Poison Ivy watched Batman's progress. She had known that Batman would appear, and she was ready for him.

"Congratulations! You've made it through the maze. Here is your prize," she exclaimed.

Suddenly, Batman was ambushed by two tree people. The
hero reached for his Utility Belt, preparing to pull out one
of his many weapons. But then he remembered that the
towering trees were the poor people transformed by Ivy's
toxin. He couldn't hurt them.

"You Gothamites think you can do whatever you want to
the earth," Poison Ivy hissed as she ran. "The city will be
better off with all the people gone and an army of trees taking
their place. And that is exactly what will happen."

"I don't think so," Batman said. He freed himself from the tree branches and removed the grapnel gun from his Utility Belt. "I'm going to uproot your evil scheme."

Bang! The Caped Crusader fired the grapnel at the fleeing villain. A super-strong wire launched through the air. It hit Poison Ivy, wrapping around her like a vine.

"I will finish the job! You cannot stop me!" she called, desperately searching for a way to escape.

"There are safer ways to protect the environment, Ivy!" Batman said.

While the police took Poison Ivy to headquarters, Batman raced back to the Batcave. He needed to find an antidote for all the people who had been harmed.

Searching quickly through the data on his high-tech Batcomputer, the hero found a solution. With Alfred's help, the antidote was ready within hours.

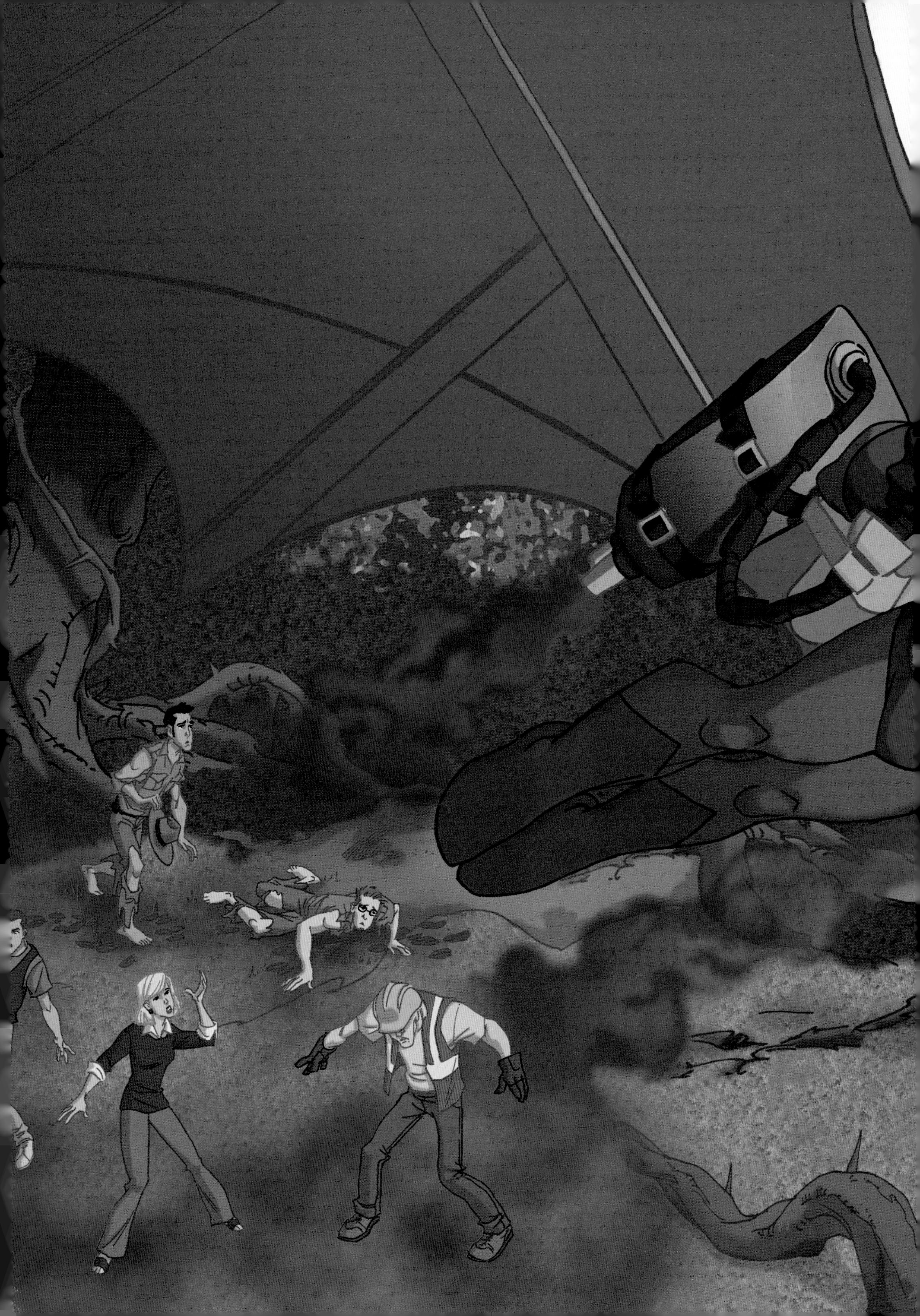

As night began to fall, Batman took to the skies in his Bat-Glider. From high above, he sprayed the entire park with the antidote.

Slowly, the trees shed their branches, and their roots began to move. They scratched their heads with their fingers and stretched their legs. They were human again!

Back at Wayne Manor, Bruce watched the local news. "Thanks to a generous donation by Wayne Enterprises, today we turn Harris Park into a forest reserve for all the people of Gotham City to enjoy for generations!" the mayor declared as he cut a bright red ribbon.

"A much better place to visit than a mall," Bruce said. Alfred couldn't help but agree.

BATMAN™

THE PRINCE OF PUZZLES

Inside Wayne Manor, Gotham City's most powerful people had gathered. Wealthy businessman Bruce Wayne stood in front of them on a large stage. "Welcome, everyone," Bruce said. "Tonight, I honor one of Gotham City's finest: Police Commissioner James Gordon."

The crowd applauded with excitement as Gordon joined Bruce on stage.

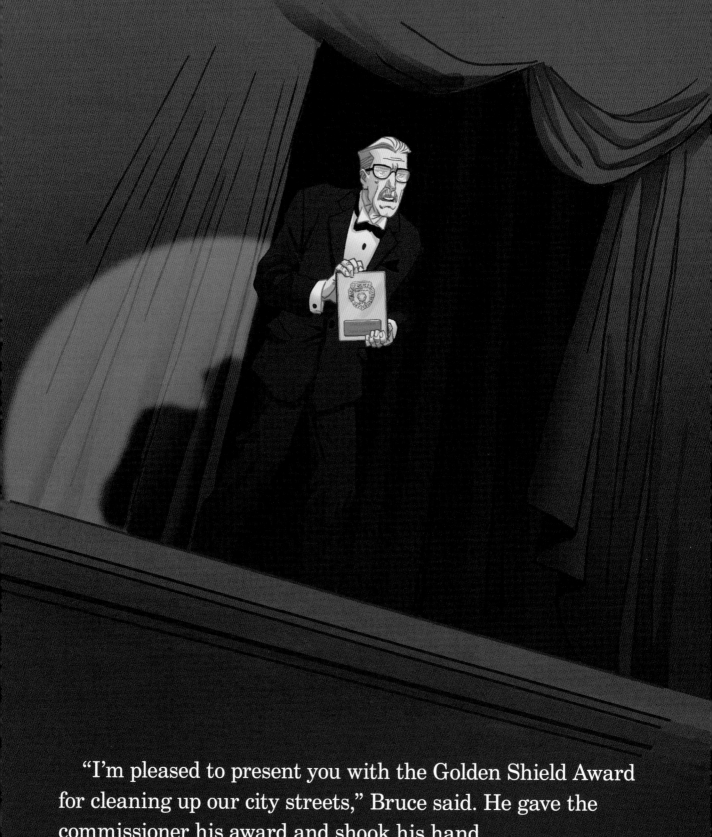

"I'm pleased to present you with the Golden Shield Award for cleaning up our city streets," Bruce said. He gave the commissioner his award and shook his hand.

"Thank you, Bruce," said Gordon. "In fact, I want to thank everyone for their support, especially my loving daughter." He scanned the crowd. "Where are you, Barbara?"

"Is that a riddle?" asked a voice in the crowd. "I love riddles, Commissioner!" The crowd parted to reveal a man standing in the middle of the room. It was the Riddler—the Prince of Puzzles. He pushed through the partygoers and stormed onto the stage, waving his question-mark cane.

"Where would a teenage girl go on a night like tonight?" the Riddler asked. "Why, shopping, of course!"

The villain
flicked his wrist, and
green smoke exploded from his cane.
Booom!
Seconds later, the smoke was gone—along with Gordon and
the Riddler!

As the other guests raced for the exits, Bruce approached his butler, Alfred. He knew Bruce's secret identity.

"Prepare the Batmobile," said Bruce.

"Have you already solved the Riddler's clue, sir?" Alfred asked.

"Of course," Bruce replied. "The best place to shop is where you'll find the most *sales*."

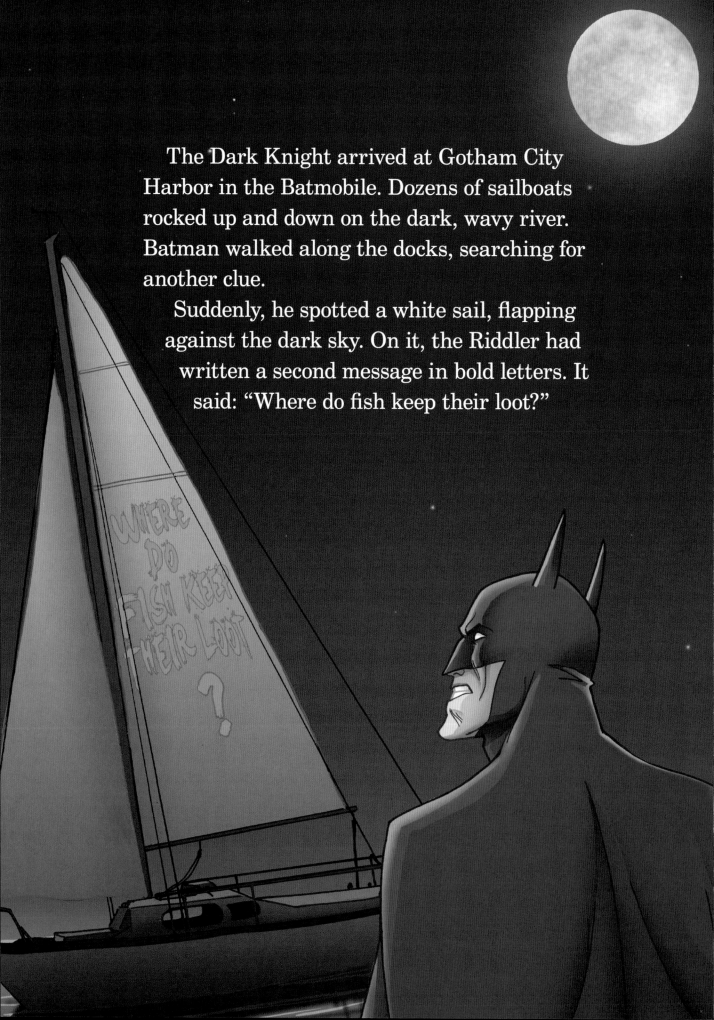

The Dark Knight arrived at Gotham City Harbor in the Batmobile. Dozens of sailboats rocked up and down on the dark, wavy river. Batman walked along the docks, searching for another clue.

Suddenly, he spotted a white sail, flapping against the dark sky. On it, the Riddler had written a second message in bold letters. It said: "Where do fish keep their loot?"

"That riddle's easy," Batman said. "Fish keep money in a river*bank*."

The Dark Knight climbed down a steep bank to the edge of the Gotham River. There, written on the muddy shore, was the third clue of the night. "The more you take," it read, "the more you leave behind."

The World's Greatest Detective knew the answer immediately. "Footprints!" he exclaimed.

Batman followed a trail of footprints to a large drainpipe. There, the hero flipped on his night-vision goggles and crept inside. The high-tech goggles allowed him to see in the pitch-dark pipe.

The pipe led to a dark chamber with steel doors on all four sides.

Suddenly, the doors slammed shut, trapping the super hero inside. Etched on one door was another clue. "What can you swallow that can also swallow you?" it read.

"Water," the Dark Knight grumbled.

The ankle-deep muck began to rise. It quickly reached the hero's neck, threatening to swallow him up. Batman stood on his tiptoes, stretching and struggling for every last breath.

Just then, another steel door opened. The water rushed out of the chamber, taking Batman along for a ride. He slid to a stop at the feet of Batgirl, his heroic sidekick.

"Good to see you, Barbara," he said, knowing the teen's secret identity. "Where were you?"

"I left the party for a moment," Batgirl replied. "When I came back, everyone was gone." She held up a high-tech device. "So I tracked my father's phone."

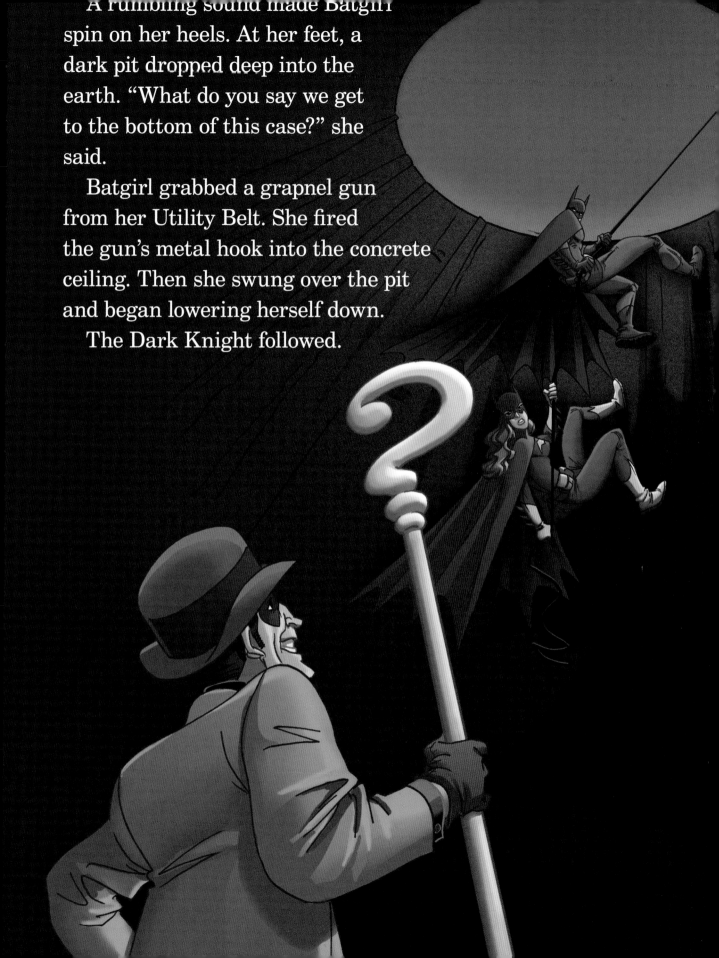

A rumbling sound made Batgirl spin on her heels. At her feet, a dark pit dropped deep into the earth. "What do you say we get to the bottom of this case?" she said.

Batgirl grabbed a grapnel gun from her Utility Belt. She fired the gun's metal hook into the concrete ceiling. Then she swung over the pit and began lowering herself down.

The Dark Knight followed.

As the heroes neared the bottom, a voice echoed in the darkness. “Well, well,” said the Riddler, “Batman’s got brains after all.”

The Riddler stood in the watery bottom of the pit. The commissioner sat behind him on a ledge with his hands tied up. Batman and Batgirl hovered above the floor on their Batropes.

“When the streets are clean, there’s still scum in the sewers,” said Batman. “Now give us the commissioner.”

“Hang in there,” joked the Riddler. “I have one last surprise!”

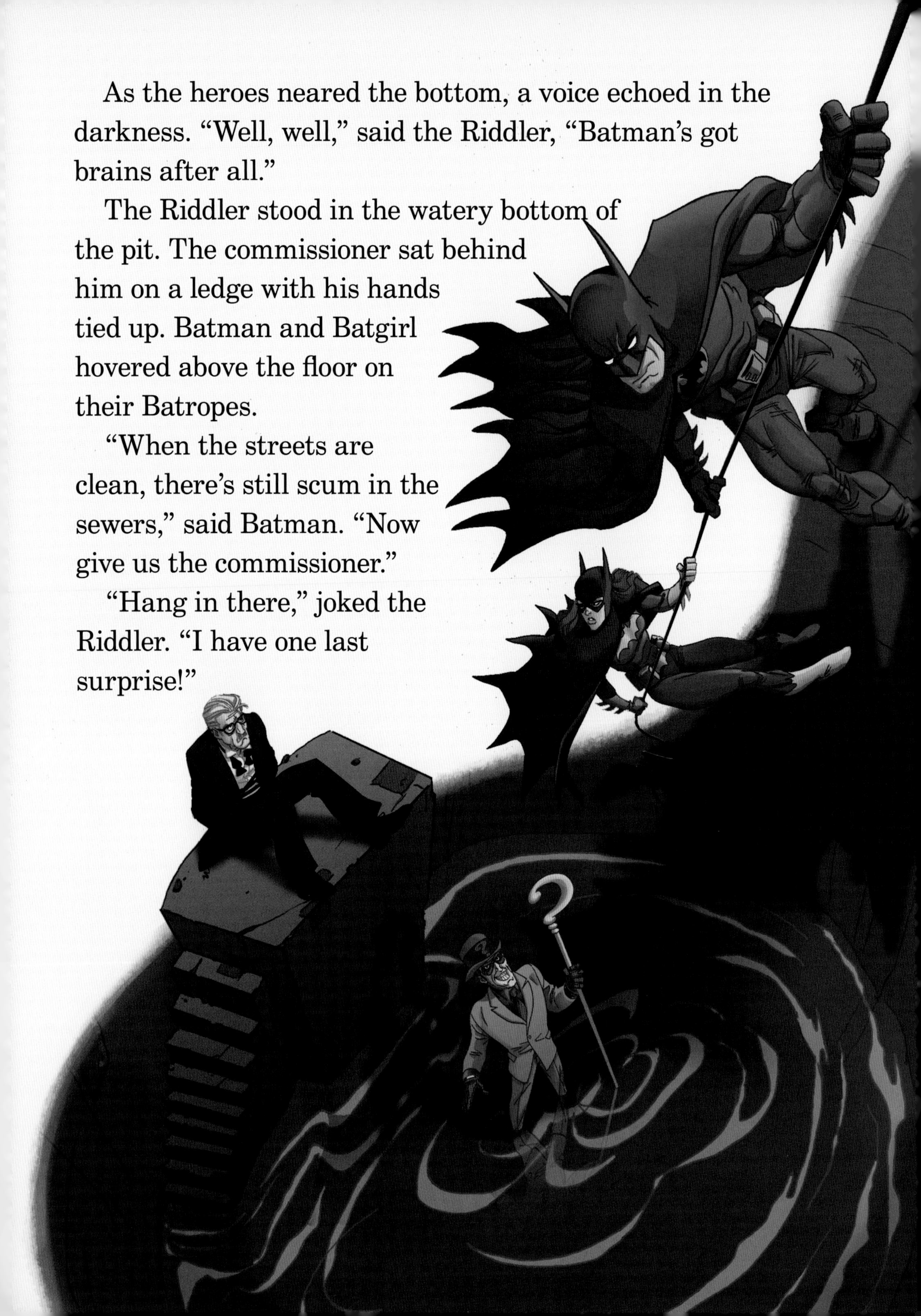

The Riddler raised his deadly cane. *Bzzz!* He fired an
electric bolt. Batman and Batgirl both swung to the side to
avoid the deadly blast.

The bolt struck the floor instead, hitting the water below their feet. Electricity jolted everything on the ground, including the Riddler! The villain passed out on the floor.

A few moments later, the heroes lowered themselves down. "The Riddler was right," Batman said. "That was certainly a surprise."

Batgirl nodded. "Yes, I believe he even shocked himself," she joked. She handcuffed the Riddler.

Batman untied Gordon and helped him out of the pit.

"Thank you, Batman," Gordon said. The commissioner turned to Batgirl, but the teen hero was already gone.

"Where did Batgirl go?" Gordon asked.

Above their heads, Batman heard the Batcycle speed away from the scene. The Dark Knight smiled.

"That, Commissioner," he said, "is a riddle even I can't solve."

BATMAN

BATTLE IN THE BATCAVE

On a cold winter night, an explosion shook the streets of downtown Gotham City. *Boom!* Within moments, the red-and-blue lights of police cars lit up the scene.

Commissioner James Gordon and several other officers quickly exited their vehicles. Near a burning building stood a large, masked figure.

"Freeze!" shouted Gordon. Behind him, a half-dozen police officers raised their weapons.

The flames of the burning building grew brighter and brighter. The man stepped closer to the police officers. "But things are just heating up, Commissioner," he said, letting out a wicked laugh.

Suddenly, from high above the city, Batman swooped to the ground on his Batrope. The super hero landed in front of his worst enemy. "Bane," he grumbled.

"You remember me, Batman," the super-villain said. He clenched his hand into a fist and cracked his knuckles. "Unfortunately, you will soon be forgotten."

Bane leaped at the Dark Knight with all his might. The super hero easily dodged the hulking brute using his expert martial arts skills.

Batman snatched a bola from his Utility Belt. He twirled the weapon above his head and then flung it at Bane. The rope flew through the air. It twisted around the villain's ankles, sending him to the ground with a loud thud.

"The bigger they are, the harder they fall," the hero said.

Just then, the wind shifted, and a thick cloud of smoke filled the air. For a moment, Batman was blinded. He choked and coughed, unable to breathe. When the smoke finally cleared, the cover of an open manhole rested on the street in front of him. Bane was gone!

A few days later, Batman sat inside the Batcave. The top secret hideout was hidden deep below Bruce Wayne's mansion. It contained hundreds of gadgets and weapons, as well as Batman's collection of crime-fighting evidence.

The Dark Knight stared at a high-tech map on the Batcomputer. "Bane couldn't have gotten far," the super hero said to himself. "The sewer pipes are dead ends, except for the one leading to this location."

"I'd call this a dead end as well," said a voice from behind Batman. "At least for one of us."

The super hero turned and spotted Bane on the other side of the Batcave. "How did you find this place?" he asked, surprised.

"A few days in the dark and you learn to follow your instincts," Bane replied. "Like a bat, I suppose."

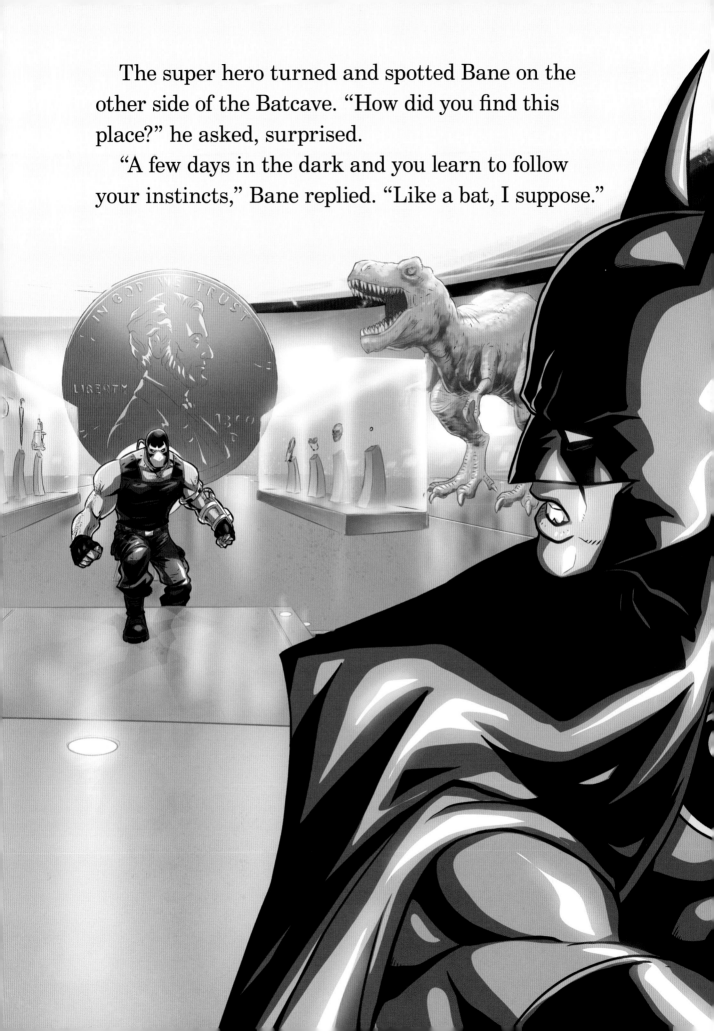

Batman stood from his chair and moved toward his enemy. "This cave only has room for one," he said, raising a single finger in the air.

"How about we flip for it?" the villain suggested. Bane lifted Batman's giant penny. He hurled the two-ton coin at the hero. *Whoosh!*

The Dark Knight jumped high to avoid the large coin, flipping forward through the air. The giant penny crashed into a glass display case. The gadgets and weapons of a dozen criminals spilled out onto the floor.

Bane quickly grabbed the Penguin's umbrella off the ground. He pressed a button on the handle, and a fireball exploded through the cave.

Batman twirled and blocked the flame with his fireproof cape. Then he flung a Batarang at the villain, who swatted away the metal weapon like it was a pesky moth.

Bane tossed the umbrella aside and picked up a question-mark cane. The weapon had once belonged to Gotham's cleverest crook, the Riddler.

"Riddle me this," Bane joked. "How did the bat feel when he lost his cave?"

"Shocked!" Bane quickly answered. He fired an electric bolt at Batman. *Zrrrt!* The bolt struck the hero! Electricity jolted through his body, stunning him. Batman stumbled but managed to keep his balance.

Then Bane grabbed another weapon from the floor.
It was the Joker's mallet. "Looks like I'll have the last
laugh today," he said.

Whoosh! Whoosh! The villain swung the mallet back
and forth at Batman. The dazed super hero dodged the
blow. Bane swung and missed, again and again.

"Strike three!" shouted a voice. On the other side of the Batcave stood Robin, Batman's teenage sidekick. He held Mr. Freeze's ray gun.

Bane lowered the mallet and turned toward Robin. "Where are your manners, Boy Wonder?" he said. "Don't you know better than to interrupt the grown-ups?"

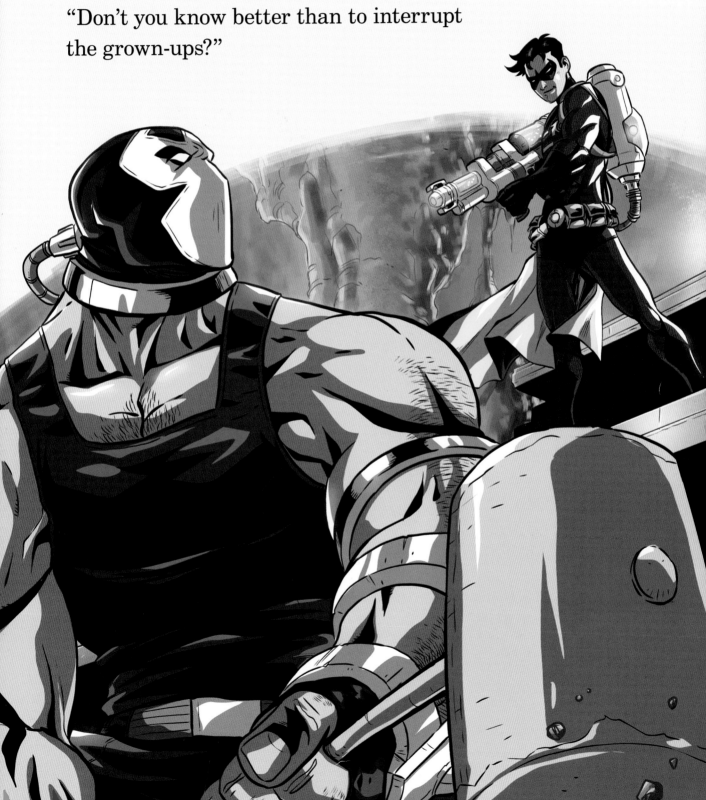

Robin raised the freeze gun. "For a cold-blooded crook, you're a real hothead," he said. "Time to chill out."
Bzzzt! Robin fired an icy blast at the super-villain.
In an instant, Bane froze into a solid block of ice.

Batman thanked his young partner. "You never were an early bird," the hero joked.

"You're right, Batman," Robin agreed, "but I always catch the crook."

Later at Arkham Asylum, the Dynamic Duo met with Police Commissioner James Gordon. "Great work, you two," he said. "Bane doesn't remember a thing, but he'll have plenty of time to think in here."

"Sounds like a bad case of brain freeze, if you ask me," Robin said with a smile.